E. Cornelia Knight

Marcus Flaminius

A View of the Military, Political and Social Life of the Romans

E. Cornelia Knight

Marcus Flaminius
A View of the Military, Political and Social Life of the Romans

ISBN/EAN: 9783742808707

Manufactured in Europe, USA, Canada, Australia, Japa

Cover: Foto ©Andreas Hilbeck / pixelio.de

Manufactured and distributed by brebook publishing software
(www.brebook.com)

E. Cornelia Knight

Marcus Flaminius

MARCUS FLAMINIUS;

OR, A VIEW OF THE

MILITARY, POLITICAL, AND SOCIAL LIFE

OF THE

ROMANS;

IN

A SERIES OF LETTERS

FROM A PATRICIAN TO HIS FRIEND;

IN THE YEAR DCC.LXII

FROM THE FOUNDATION OF ROME,

TO THE YEAR DCC.LXIX.

BY E. CORNELIA KNIGHT.

Juſtum et tenacem propoſiti virum
Non civium ardor prava jubentium,
Non vultus inſtantis tyranni
Mente quatit ſolidâ.

HORACE, Book III. Ode iii.

LONDON:

PRINTED FOR C. DILLY, IN THE POULTRY.

M.DCC.XCII.

MARCUS FLAMINIUS;

OR, THE
LIFE OF THE ROMANS.

MARCUS TO SEPTIMUS.

AS I was concluding my last letter, Drusus entered and conjured me, if I should discover any thing relative to the retreat of Valerius, to give him the earliest intelligence; assuring me that he would not be undeserving of my confidence, but unite his efforts with mine, to remove any obstacles that might obstruct the return of my uncle. I thanked him for his zeal, but answered only in general terms; for it is not probable, my friend, that Valerius would approve that I should communicate to the son of Tibe-

B

rius

rius the afylum he may have chofen; at the fame time I am perfuaded that Drufus interefts himfelf warmly and fincerely in the reftoration of Valerius.

Though it was impracticable to keep my intention wholly concealed, yet, as I wifhed to make my journey as privately as poffible, I have taken with me few fervants, but among them is a Sicilian flave, perfectly acquainted with the country, whom Germanicus advifed me to receive into my family: he is remarkably intelligent, and may be confiderably ufeful in my prefent refearches. Before my departure I took leave of Manfred, who will foon be reftored to his native foil. I charged him to enquire into the fate of Sigifmar, and to give me information of him, his mother, and brother.

I am now at Capua*, where I hoped to receive fome intelligence of Valerius; but

---

* Modern Capua is two miles diftant from the ancient city, of which fome ruins ftill remain. The country is remarkably fertile.

not

not having fucceeded in my expection, I
fhall immediately fet out for Baiæ: my
journey would have been very delightful, if
anxiety for the object of my fearch, and the
uncertainty of the event, did not engrofs my
mind.✝ The aftonifhing beauty of the neighbourhood of this celebrated city has in fome
meafure awakened my attention. I am unwilling to think that virtue is wholly dependent on climate and other exterior circumftances; but our Roman colonifts begin
to imitate the manners of the ancient inhabitants, and if ever feducing pleafure and
indolent apathy were excufable, it would be
in the foft plains of Campania. Bounteous
nature feems here to render induftry unneceffary: the purfuits of active life are fcarcely
to be expected in a place, the air of which
lulls and enervates every faculty of the foul.
Hannibal robbed us of great part of the
glory of driving him from Italy by yielding to the allurements of this city: I am

 jealous

jealous for the honour even of such an enemy, and lament that it should have been. lost amidst these myrtle and orange groves, which remind me of his shame. What most astonishes me is, that this should ever have been the seat of dominion of a free and powerful republic. The people appear born for slavery and dissipation: their gaiety is without a motive, and rather apparent than real: their features are regular, but they have nothing thinking or animated; and their character seems a perfect contrast with that of the Cheruscans. They would mutually despise each. other, not considering that the extremes of luxury and barbarism are no otherwise different in their effects, than the cup of poison and the dagger.

Soft music resounds through the street; sumptuous repasts are given on the terraces of the houses, lighted by innumerable torches; the porticos re-echo with the feet of the dancers, and the loud acclamations of the spectators.

spectators. On one side I hear the vociferous clamour of wretches deceived by the inconstant dice, and on the other the authoritative voice of the guard imposing a truce on turbulence or diffention. Unhappy Campanians! they pafs their lives without knowing the value or even the pleafure of their exiftence. On every countenance I perceive the manifeft fymptoms of liftlefs indifference. Surely I could never be feduced by the boafted delights of Capua; and yet, whoever once becomes their votary, is incapable of any future exertion.

Drufus has here a confiderable number of gladiators *, maintained and inftructed at his expenfe. This cruel and humiliating employment, only to be defended by a pretence that fuch ferocious fpectacles are an incitement to the courage of the people, exhibits no real proof of their intrepidity. The man who will for the amufement of others attack

* Tacitus, and other hiftorians,

his

his fellow creature without provocation, neither deserves praise, nor even the sordid gain which is lavishly bestowed on him. The courage of a brave people wants not to be excited by the view of mercenary combatants; and to grace such wretches with the arms of a soldier, is to degrade the honour of the defenders of their country. You could not, my dear Septimus, better employ the influence you possess over the mind of Drusus, than in dissuading him from such spectacles. These gladiators, you well know, are unhappy men trained up to ferocity; not only useless, but disgraceful to their country; incapable, should they ever be wanted, of supporting the laborious duties to which their birth had allotted them. Is it not painful to humanity and reason to see men of courage and education interest themselves in the event of a combat between the lowest of mankind, whom they have perhaps excited to mutual destruction, from no other motive

than

than to fill up a vacant hour of their own existence, which satiety of pleasure has rendered tedious? I thank heaven my time never lingers while I can hope to be useful to my friends or to the republic.

Were I certain of the destiny of Valerius, every step would afford some new object to gratify my curiosity, or to awaken remembrance. I have shaken off the chains of love, and am no follower of ambition, except when founded on duty. I flatter myself with having acquired sufficient philosophy to be unmoved by exterior circumstances, and hope you will have no further reason to complain that my ardent imagination, though it often gives me transport, never allows me serenity. Could I once more embrace the man whom I love and venerate with filial regard, his affection and the friendship of Septimus would constitute the future happiness of my life.

LETTER

WHAT a day have I paſſed ! how deeply have I been affected, my dear Septimius, with the ſolitary and deſert aſpect of the ſuperb villa of my beloved, my reſpected uncle! This part of the country is unknown to you; and I, who am happy in imparting to you the impreſſion which objects, familiar to your remembrance, have made on my imagination, vould wiſh to ſatisfy your curioſity relative to the ſcenes which you have not yet beheld. But I know not where to begin my deſcription; my heart has been more engaged than my eyes, and my impatience to arrive at a place where I hoped to receive information of Valerius, and where every object would recall him to my idea, made

me

me indifferent to thofe interefting fcenes that prefented themfelves to my fight in the way from Capua hither.

I have found this neglected villa inhabited by an ancient freedman, whofe fidelity to his abfent mafter remains fuperior to every other confideration. A few flaves under his directions preferve the gardens from total neglect; but the greater number, by order of the magiftrates, who have interefted themfelves in the affairs of my uncle, are diftributed in various houfes of the Valerian family, until fome knowledge can be obtained of the future intentions of Titus *.

The old man met me at the beginning of the plantations, and wept bitterly when, after telling my name, I enquired into the myfterious departure of Valerius. He told me that his patron had one evening, as was often his cuftom, fet out for Naples with Valeria and a few attendants, acquainting

* Titus Valerius.

his

his family that he should return the night after; but that, to the great surprise of his servants, no intelligence was received of him the next or the following day; that, on the third morning from his departure, one of the slaves who had accompanied him appeared, and related that his master, instead of entering Naples, had crossed the country towards Brundusium, and, at a day's journey from this place had commanded him to return and warn his household not to be surprised if he and Valeria should be long absent, as particular reasons induced him to leave Italy for some months, but that when expedient he would give them further intelligence of his designs. I asked to see the slave who had been dispatched by Valerius, but was told he died suddenly soon after his return.

The freedman requested that I would enter the house and repose myself. " You will not," said he, " find either the apart-

ments

ments or the gardens in the state I would wish; but what is the body when the soul is fled? I watch over the remains as diligently as age and sorrow will permit me; but every hour my strength decreases, and my grief augments."

In the vestibule I found the statues of the Muses, and the best of our most celebrated orators and poets. On entering the supper-hall, I observed the figure of Harpocrates near the door; and, in three niches, the statues of Ceres, Bacchus, and Pomona. The same number of basso-reliefs represented Baucis and Philemon; Admetus, though overwhelmed with grief, receiving Hercules; and Scipio, with Asdrubal, at the table of Syphax.

My attention was particularly attracted by the library, in which Valerius has collected the works of all the learned whose studies have enriched the public; but no busts of philosophers decorate the room. The portrait

trait of the good King Evander *, who firſt introduced the knowledge of letters into Italy, is the only one to be ſeen in this apartment. The books are neatly but not oſtentatiouſly ornamented; thoſe which have no other merit than acuteneſs of inveſtigation, brilliant ideas, or elegant language, are placed at a conſiderable height, while thoſe which inculcate hiſtorical truths, uſeful ſciences, or ſound morality, are neareſt the hand, and open to all who enter the library. Adjoining to it is the chamber of Valerius—O Septimus! you will feel for me, you will conceive the ſenſations with which I entered it! On a ſmall table, near the bed, lay the ſayings of Socrates, and Virgil's Georgics. Two ſtatues on ſimilar pedeſtals are placed in the room; one repreſents the lovely and elegant figure of Valeria as a child, and the other is a portrait of myſelf with the bulla * about my neck, as I

* Livy, Book 1.

† An ornament worn about the neck of the Roman children. Ainſworth.

remember

remember it was taken not long before my firſt campaign in Dalmatia—excellent man! with what tendernefs he loved me!

From this chamber we entered an apartment, where my faithful guide informed me that his maſter uſed to ſtudy. The walls are adorned with various ſmall pictures on a dark ground, all finiſhed to perfection: the drawing is correct, the draperies are light and tranſparent, the attitudes elegant, and the colouring, which is as ſlight as poſſible, peculiarly harmonious. Theſe are the work of Valeria, and repreſent ſeveral intereſting ſubjects in the Roman hiſtory. Among the reſt are the death of Virginia; the Sabine wives interpoſing between their huſbands and parents to ſtop their reciprocal fury, and the Roman ladies preſenting their gold and ornaments to the public treaſury. In this room are the buſts of Naſica and Cato the Cenſor. I could not look on them without reflecting on the impartial virtues of their owner:

owner: ever influenced by a difinterefted love for his country, he has divefted himfelf of party prejudice, and efteems all thofe who would truly contribute to the welfare of Rome, however they may differ in opinion concerning the meafures moft conducive to it.

The apartments of his daughter are fimple and elegant. I here contemplated with unfpeakable delight and emotion, the portrait of my mother in a diftinguifhed fituation. Had I vifited the tombs of all who are, or ever were dear to me, I could not have been differently affected from what I felt in wandering over the habitation where dwelt this great, this beft of men. I cannot enter into a detail of the apartments deftined for his friends; they are far more fplendid than his own, or thofe of Valeria. You know his heart was liberal and beneficent to all.

The gardens prefent an appearance not uninftructive for the neighbourhood of Baiæ, where

where health is ufually a pretence for diffi-
pation, and where the rural beauties of
nature infpire as little the love of fimple and
refined pleafures as the moft magnificent and
populous capital. The gardens of Valerius are
difpofed in a manner fuitable to the nature of
the ground; Oppofite to the houfe is a grove
of plane trees, and evergreen oaks, through
which flows a fmall rivulet, having on one
fide a plain, and on the other a lofty hill.
In the middle of the grove appears a ftatue of
young Alcides in a thoughtful attitude, as
feeming to meditate on his important choice.
Befide the rivulet are ferpentine walks bor-
dered with flowers of every hue, whofe
lively colours and delightful perfumes give
inexpreffible charms to the place. A path
diverfified by elegant feats, garlands of vine
hanging from tree to tree, fhady arbours,
and ftatues of Fauns and Driads, leads to a
theatre of fumptuous architecture, in which
the Corinthian order is moft confpicuous.

Here,

Here, as I was told, Valerius ufed to entertain his friends, and many of the neighbouring inhabitants with reprefentations of the
beft and moft inftructive dramatic pieces, as
well ferious as comic. A few days before
his departure his comedians had performed
feveral Greek plays, written by Germanicus
with great tafte and genius. Beyond the
theatre is a circus, and a magnificent ban-
queting room, adorned with paintings of
ineftimable value, and a variety of beautiful
ftatues, particularly a Cupid mounted on a
lion, that he governs by the found of the
harp. Beyond this building is an enclofure
wholly formed of myrtles and rofes, fo
high as to conceal from the windows the
view of the country beyond it; but when you
approach nearer to it, you perceive a fearful
precipice ending in a vaft cavity where no
vegetation appears. The ground is here a
pale yellow, and bears the marks of fubterranean fire; it refounds hollow beneath

the

the feet, while a dark fmoke rifes at inter-
vals above the furface ; and the natives give
it the name of the Forum of Vulcan*.   Further, the eye commands a diftant view of
the Avernian lake, and the marfhy and defo-
late plains near Cuma.

Quitting this aweful profpect and returning
to the ftatue of Alcides in the grove of plane
trees, I followed the other path which leads
up the hill.   The afcent is fteep, and the
entangled branches feem negligently left to
embarrafs the wanderer,   through a way
rocky and difficult of accefs.   Between the
trees appeared various ftatues of hydras, chimæras, fphinxes, and other fabulous animals.
Coming out of the wood, I perceived the
cafcade which forms the rivulet ; it falls
from a confiderable elevation, and makes a
ftriking contraft between the filvery bright-
nefs of the fpray, and the dark colouring of
the rocks.   A bridge of the boldeft con-

* The Forum of Vulcan, Solfatare.

C   ftruction

struction is thrown acrofs the stream, and the passing stranger is almost deafened by the noise of the falling waters, while the bridge trembles under his feet: having passed it, he finds himself in a dark grove of lofty cypresses, whose venerable appearance proves them to have long been tenants of the mountain. Here I perceived sepulchral urns and tombs of various forms, amidst these funereal trees, dedicated to the memory of those who have died in the pursuit of honourable fame. One bears the name of Regulus, another of the Decii, and a third of Curtius, with a striking alto-relievo, in which he appears on horseback leaping into the gulph: a fourth bears an inscription, and representation of Lucius Emilius Paulus seated on a stone after the battle of Cannæ, and refusing the horse of the young Roman who leaves him with every mark of anguish in his countenance. At the furthest part of the grove I observed a most beautiful urn of Parian marble,

marble, to which I was directed by the vivid green of a fmall plantation of laurels, that fhaded it towards the eaft, while to the weft the pedeftal is covered by rofes, woodbine, and various flowers. On a near approach I read the following infcription, which I entreat you not to fhew to any of your friends; but which I cannot refift communicating to Septimius, as a proof of the partial affection of Valerius.

TO THE MANES
OF
MARCUS QUINTIUS FLAMINIUS,
SON OF MARCUS AND VALERIA,
WHOSE INTELLECTUAL ENDOWMENTS
COULD ONLY BE EXCEEDED
BY
HIS PROBITY, GENEROSITY, AND VALOUR;
WHOSE FORM WAS AS DISTINGUISHED AS
HIS VIRTUES.
HE FELL IN THE CAUSE OF HONOUR
AND HIS COUNTRY
ON THE FIELD OF TEUTOBURGIUM.

O Septimius! how much did Valerius

promife to himfelf from his nephew! how great muft have been his affliction!

This urn has not only convinced me more than ever of his affection, but has made me turn my reflections on myfelf, and impartially confider how far I am unde-ferving of thefe praifes. I am confcious that the world cannot reproach me with a want either of probity, or courage; but where are thefe mental endowments, thefe diftin-guifhed virtues, with which the indulgence of a parent has honoured me? Have I not neg-lected opportunities of improving my mind and being ufeful to my fellow citizens? Have I not often been fatisfied with feeling the emotions of benevolence, and with ad-miring the talents of the learned? Hence-forth let me endeavour to practife what till now, I fear, I have only approved, or this urn will be a monument of the partiality of Valerius, and of the unworthinefs of Marcus.

The

The grove of cypresses ends in a long walk of the same trees, which leads to an open temple with Ionic columns, on the summit of the hill; in the middle is an altar of porphyry, on which is placed the statue of Immortality, and in the freeze above the entrance is a medallion with the figure of Virtue supported by Constancy, and crowned by Fame. The temple is surrounded with laurels, except where a space is left between the two furthest columns, commanding the most delightful prospect: the Elysian Fields* appear immediately beneath the hill; the mount Misenum, with the Roman gallies stationed near it, and various smaller vessels failing lightly on the placid surface of the gulph of Baiæ; the verdant island of Prochyte, and the blue conical hills of Inarime †; on the other side Nisida, whose rocks are

* Still named Campi Elisi, near Baiæ.

† Isle of Ischia.

C 3

crowned

crowned with groves; the coaft adorned
with villas; the ftately fabricks of Naples
rifing majeftically above the intermediate
promontory; behind, the lofty Vefuvius
covered with vineyards, and the long chain
of the diftant Apennines terminating in the
Cape of Minerva; the purple tints of
Caprea uniting with an horizon of gold, and
the foft exhalations that flutter in the azure
fky—all contribute to form a fcene which
fancy cannot embellifh! I quitted with pain
this enchanting fpot, and returned to the
houfe immerfed in grief for the abfence of
him, whofe feeling heart and liberal hand
had animated the natural beauties of the
place. I here found many of the neighbouring nobility and Roman knights, who,
having heard of my arrival, came to enquire
after Valerius All fpoke of him with tender veneration, all regretted his departure,
and fought in vain to account for it. I could

fcarce

scarce refrain from tears, my heart bled with anguifh, and yet I was ftill more affected when I perceived the portico crowded with poor citizens, who had experienced his bounty, and were now reduced to indigence. They did not feem to claim my protection; they only wifhed to learn the fate of their benefactor. At this fight, Septimius! my heart affured me that the abfence of Valerius could not be voluntary; he would not have left without provifion thofe whofe comforts, and almoft whofe being depended on his charity. My mind is involved in doubts and perplexities: I fhall fleep here this night, or rather I fhall continue till the break of day permits my departure, for fleep-muft here be a ftranger to me.

I wander through the rooms and galleries; while my agitated mind has found no reft, except when I have been addreffing thefe lines to you. O Septimius! I fhall

C 4

not

not enjoy a moment's peace till I have met with my beloved protector. I dare not think that he is no more—that idea would drive me to madnefs.

AFTER concluding the letter which I wrote to you the night before laſt, I recollected that Manlius Torquatus, præfect of the navy at Miſenum, was an intimate friend of Valerius; and I thought it my duty to make him a viſit, and enquire whether he knew any circumſtances relative to the departure of my uncle. He received me with tranſport, and, though he could not give me the information I deſired, inſiſted on ſupplying me with a proper veſſel, and experienced mariners to conduct me to Sicily. This obliged me to delay my embarkation, and in the mean time I have experienced from him every act of attention and kindneſs. He is a man of real and diſtinguiſhed

merit,

merit, and has acquired the higheft reputation, as commander of the fleet, ftationed here by Auguftus to keep the weftern provinces in fubjection. He is efteemed by the officers, adored by the feamen, and beloved as a father by the navy in general: he maintains the exacteft difcipline, and excites the moft active emulation. His table is fumptuous and hofpitable: nothing can equal the graceful hilarity with which he prefides over it; for he confiders cheerfulnefs as abfolutely neceffary in his profeffion, and often cites the example of Duilius, who ufed to be accompanied home from fupper with the flute and harp. You have perhaps heard, that when he was only twenty years of age, he fought on the fide of Marc Anthony at the battle of Actium; and he is faid to have behaved with remarkable intrepidity. After the death of the Triumvir he became the friend of Agrippa, for whofe memory he has a high veneration, and to whofe inftruc-

tions,

tions and example he is chiefly indebted for his profeffional knowledge. Yet not-withftanding this advantage, and the favour of Auguftus which he enjoyed, he never forgot the fentiments of gratitude with which his firft leader had infpired him, but openly avowed himfelf the champion of his fame, at a time when Octavius was as anxious to obliterate the remembrance of his actions, as he had been to rob him of his dignity and power. Torquatus ftill retains the fame principles; and though nothing can be more difpleafing to the prefent emperor, he continues to fpeak of Marc Anthony as a brave, generous, and affectionate commander; while even thofe who wear the name of this much injured man, obferve carefully the rigorous filence, which has been enjoined them by the reigning party.

You may imagine that I am not in a ftate of mind to partake of the focial amufements which Torquatus would prepare for me. I

could

could not however refuse to comply in some
measure with his request, and to visit with
him the magnificent villa* of the emperor,
which formerly belonged to Lucullus, and
the more simple dwellings of Marius and
Cæsar the Dictator. Near the latter is the
Temple of Venus †, an elegant structure, at
a small distance from the superb edifice consecrated to Mercury ‡. But what particularly
engaged my attention, and what Manlius
shewed me with the greatest pleasure, is the
noble reservoir ‖, constructed by Agrippa for
the use of the fleet while he commanded on this
station. This immense structure is supported
by arches, incrusted with a composition as
hard as marble, and susceptible of the highest
polish: it is happily placed under Mount

* Phædrus, &c. Very little remains of the numerous
and splendid villas near Baiæ and Misenum; there are
some ruins in the sea, which are still called La Casa di
Lucullo.

† Temples of Venus and ‡ Mercury, supposed to be
those still existing.

‖ The ruins of this are still very interesting.

Misenum,

Mifenum, ferving not only to fupply the navy, but likewife the neighbouring towns with frefh water, an article of peculiar value in this country.

Towards evening we went to Puteoli*, where a temple is raifing to the memory of Auguftus, in the moft elevated part of the city: the architecture is of the Corinthian order, and will be very beautiful. We vifited the buildings and groves †, which Cicero ufed to call his Academy, yet I believe that Manlius would not have fhewn them to me, but at my particular requeft: he does not love the mention of Cicero, and is greatly difpleafed if any one fpeaks of his death. I was fo inadvertent as to begin the converfation, and immediately perceived the pain it gave him.

* Pozzuolo. The infcriptions on the temple and feveral of the columns remain. It is now the cathedral.

† Cicero's villa is ftill fhewn at Pozzuolo, near the entrance of the town.

“ The

" The death of Cicero," said he, " does not justify his Philippics; but it has drawn a veil over many of the illiberal and unjust aspersions with which they abound.   There seems to have been a fatality in the persecution which Marc Anthony never ceased to experience from this attractive orator: an ill construction was put on all his words and actions: his friends were seduced; his enemies exasperated; his follies exaggerated, and his virtues forgotton.   The law of self-preservation appears to have authorised his resentment; but this resentment has cast a greater odium on his name, than if he had proscribed a thousand honester men unendowed with the dangerous gift of eloquence.

He must surely have been misled: had he merely consulted his own generosity and magnanimity, he would have pardoned his implacable enemy, and have risen superior to him; but now the victory remains with Cicero: his writings, not his arm, were
formidable

formidable to the Triumvir, and they will probably exift as long as literature has any votaries. They will deceive pofterity as they did the contemporaries of the orator: the fentiments and diction will be admired without any inveftigation of the motives from which they fprung, and few will be impartial enough to form a juft eftimate of the character of Cicero from a comparifon of his oration for Marcellus with the firft he pronounced after that parricide, to which he inftigated men, not lefs ungrateful, but more daring than himfelf. He deferved to be facrificed to the manes of Julius Cæfar; he had flattered and betrayed him; but Anthony was too much the object of his hatred to become his punifher—yet, alas! which of us can fay with certainty how far clemency fhould be extended, or how far we can command our refentment! I do not attribute the horrors of the profcription to the unfortunate Triumvir with whom I

ferved,

ferved, nor even to Auguftus or his colleague. Brutus, Caffius, and their adherents, were in reality the authors, becaufe they taught men by a fearful example to diftruft the profeffions of gratitude, and the ties of obligation. Cæfar fet no bounds to his forgivenefs of injuries—he was therefore murdered and deified."

Thefe laft words of Torquatus infpired me with the higheft efteem for him, and I refpected his partiality to the memory of a chief, whofe errors he endeavoured to excufe without imitating his conduct.

Puteoli is a ftrong and well-fortified town: you know that Hannibal went to facrifice at Cuma, in order to attack this place, without feeming to make it the object of his journey, and that after three days fruitlefs endeavours he was repulfed with confiderable lofs.

From Puteoli we rowed along the moft beautiful coaft that imagination can conceive ;

ceive; the rocks are covered with flowers
and aromatic plants; the variety of iflands
difperfed round the gulph, and the numerous cities which ornament the fhores, form
the moft delightful and animated profpect.
Nothing can furpafs in beauty the fituation
of Naples, except the brilliancy and variegated colouring of the fky under which it is
placed.   We arrived there late at night, and
it is impoffible to defcribe the effect of the
moon-light on this enchanting bay, which
has been celebrated by Virgil, and many
other favourites of the Mufes; and it muft
be confeffed that nothing can be more truly
poetical than the appearance. Manlius fpeaks
highly of the talents of the inhabitants, of
the warmth of their imagination, and the
gaiety of their temper.   I believe them to
be like all other Campanians, rather fonder
of pleafure, and more carelefs of fame, than
is confiftent either with their intereft or real
happinefs; but they are free from many deftruc-

D   tive

tive passions which disturb the natives of more active cities. They are neither the slaves of ambition nor of avarice: they enjoy, perhaps too eagerly, the advantages lavished on them by nature; but these they are willing to participate with others: they receive strangers with cordial hospitality, and have few enemies amidst the neighbouring cities.

Manlius, who had indeed brought me hither for that purpose, was very desirous I should be present at a theatrical representation, which the Neapolitans had prepared on account of a solemn feast. I at first declined to comply with his request, because I would not delay my departure; but the weather proving unfavourable, I was obliged to yield, and should have been highly gratified if my mind had been more at ease. The theatre is magnificent, and the music excellent: the drama was the PROMETHEUS of Efchylus: this bold and interesting composition was assisted by the uncommon merit

of

of the performers, and by all the illusion of scenery, decoration, and machinery. I do not believe that any poem ever breathed more forcibly the spirit of independence, or that liberty of principle ever approached nearer to seditious turbulence: there are some passages which made so dreadful an impression on me, that I was more than once tempted to leave the theatre. The sight of a hero, exiled and tormented by Jupiter for having studied the happiness of his fellow-creatures, and endeavoured to free them from the sufferings inflicted by despotism, bore so strong a resemblance to the image, which is for ever present to my thoughts, that I felt the most painful and oppressive sensations. What a powerful effect has poetry when it coincides with our ruling passions! It excites them to all the vehemence of enthusiasm, and makes us greater than mortals, or more desperate than madmen. I was obliged to use every effort to moderate my

senfenfations, and would have given millions never to have entered the theatre. Torquatus obferved my emotion, and, as it was early, propofed our taking a ride to Herculaneum *. This city abounds with elegant buildings, and is delightfully fituated at the foot of Mount Vefuvius. The inhabitants live in opulence and fplendor, and many artifts are employed to adorn their habitations. We went to the houfe of Nonius Balbus, where I faw an interefting buft of Plato †, and two excellent ftatues of a Fawn and a Mercury feated: Manlius intends the latter as a prefent for one of the temples. Devotion, or rather fuperftition, prevails over all this country; and fince the Egyptian divinities have been worfhipped in the cities, there is fcarcely a folly or a vice which has not been confecrated by

* This city, deftroyed by an eruption of Mount Vefuvius, and difcovered in the prefent century, is too well known to require a defcription.

† Buft and ftatues, in the King's Mufeum at Portici.

public

public adoration.   Manlius remarks, that magnificent gifts are offered to thefe divinities, in the fame belief as the Latins* formerly entertained of Jupiter, when they befought him to defend them againft the tyranny of Mezentius, if he expected they fhould beftow the firft fruits on him, and not be compelled, like the Rutulians, to offer them to the fovereign.   It is certain that the devotion of thefe people cannot be much enlightened, while they fuppofe that morality is not included in religion.   Manlius is juftly prejudiced againft Ifis, Serapis, and Anubis; he never fees the Syftrum, or the key of the Nile, without recollecting the flight of Cleopatra, and the ruin of his unfortunate commander.   We ftayed laft night at Herculaneum, and this morning vifited Pompeia †, a fmall but not unpleafing town, which, like

* Fragment of Cato.

† Pompeia met with the fame fate as Herculaneum, well known by Sir William Hamilton's defcription.

D 3

the

the former, acknowledges Alcides for its founder. At this place is a ftrong detachment of the legion appointed to ferve on board the fleet; and in the neighbourhood are country-feats belonging to many of our patricians. Hence we went to Stabia *, the ancient capital of the Ofcans, afterwards poffeffed by the Samnites, near the delightful banks of the Sarnus. The coolnefs of the breezes, the mountains that fhade the city from the burning heats of the fouth, with the groves and woods that furround it, make the fituation peculiarly eligible for fummer. The Cæfarian family have here a magnificent villa, with extenfive and beautiful gardens: at a fmall diftance are three mineral ftreams, which have their fources clofe to each other, yet are different in their qualities; and very near them is a fountain

* An ancient city, near Caftellamare, where his Sicilian Majefty has a palace delightfully fituated. Stabia is mentioned by Strabo, and feveral ancient authors.

of

of the pureft water. The fame particularity
is to be obferved in the ground: the chain
of mountains extending along the coaft, bears
no marks of the vulcanic materials that appear in Vefuvius; and at the foot of the
latter, in the bay oppofite to Stabia, rifes a
fmall ifland*, or rather a rock, of picturefque appearance, the formation of which is
faid to be totally different.

On our return, we afcended the fertile Vefuvius, and enjoyed a moft noble view of
the adjacent country, and of the beautiful
gulph of Parthenope, the fetting fun greatly
adding to the beauty of the profpect. We
perceived an infinite number of flourifhing
cities, amongft which I diftinguifhed Nola,
where the great Marcellus firft oppofed with
fuccefs the conquering arms of Hannibal,
and ftood forth the deliverer of his country,
Nola, where Auguftus breathed his laft, and

* Rovigliano, in the bay of Caftellamare. It is compofed of lime-ftone.

D 4

left

left as an inheritance to his adoptive fon the empire of the world. I did not feel myfelf difpofed to applaud the laft fcene of this important actor, but impatiently returned to Naples, in hope of embarking for Sicily.

I found a light and well armed veffel in readinefs, and am affured by Torquatus that during the night a favourable wind will fpring up, and permit my departure. I hope to fee him at fome happier period, when my mind will be more tranquil, to thank him for his kindnefs. Farewell, my friend, I fhall write to you as foon as I have any pleafing intelligence to communicate—perhaps fooner—for Heaven knows how I may fucceed in my wifhes!

LETTER

I OMITTED writing to you, my friend, on my arrival at Meſſana, and have ſince deferred from day to day informing you of my proceedings, ſince all my ſearch has hitherto been fruitleſs. I have made the moſt diligent enquiry throughout Sicily, and have been aſſiſted by the prætor, and by every Roman of note. A gloomy deſpair begins now to overwhelm me, and my future life ſeems at leaſt condemned to dreadful uncertainty, to a ſtate, the wretchedneſs of which cannot be denied even by the thoughtleſs, nor alleviated by the philoſopher. Your letter, which I have received in this iſland, enjoins me not to deſpond, though you acknowledge the little probability of my obtaining

taining any information at Baiæ. Alas! I
know not whether it was hope of fuccefs,
or fond attachment to the beloved fpot, that
conducted me thither. After the departure
of a much valued friend, we cannot refufe
ourfelves the melancholy fatisfaction of in-
dulging our grief in the places, which he
inhabited, or where we bade him adieu;
but it was natural I fhould repair to Baiæ,
as the laft place from which any account had
been received of my uncle. The death of
the flave, who accompanied him during the
firft day's journey, is indeed unfortunate;
yet what more could he have told me than
he had related to the freedman? That Valerius fhould take fo fingular, and apparently
fo fudden a refolution, is contrary to reafon;
but, on the other hand, the intelligence
which you gained from the Illyrian appears
to be decifive. The weather, you fay, was
fair, the veffel near Meffana, and no profpect
of danger—what can I fuppofe? Has he
changed his place of retreat? Some of the
inhabitants

inhabitants muft have known that he was here. Did he pafs through the ftreight, and embark on the coaft of Calabria, or on one of the neighbouring iflands? This is declared to be impoffible, an exact regifter being kept of all the fhips that fail between Rhegium and Meffana, with the paffengers they contain, which regifter I have examined, but all in vain. I know not whether to direct my courfe—and yet I never will relinquifh the purfuit.

O! had Valerius received the news that I was ftill living, he would not have fled from my filial embraces—but furely his flight was not voluntary, though it feems certain that no emiffaries from Tiberius, no friend of Sejanus appeared at the time of his departure. Forgive me, Septimius, my ideas are difordered; my imagination wanders from conjecture to conjecture; if fome pitying power does not foon extricate me from this ftate of cruel perplexity, it is impoffible I fhould retain my reafon.

Some-

Sometimes, in diftraction, I think of fly-
ing to Rome, entering the apartments of
Tiberius, and forcing him, by my juft fury,
to lay afide the mafk of diffimulation, and
declare—declare what? I have no evidence
that he has acted treacheroufly by Valerius;
and, indeed, it is fcarcely probable—muft I
add to my calamity the guilt of unjuft fufpicions!

Septimius, affift me, counfel me, fave me
from defpair!

LETTER

THE guilty secret is disclosed—O Septimius! my suspicions were not unjust; but I trust the crime has not been completed. Thanks to the immortal Ruler of the universe, I may still hope that Valerius lives; and while the winds are cruelly adverse to my impatience, I have time to inform you of what I have learned, and of the uncommon kindness, the benevolent friendship to which I owe this important intelligence.

Soon after I had dispatched my last letter, I returned to Messana, reiterated my enquiries, which ended, as before, in disappointment, and gave myself up to despondency. I avoided society, and became insensible of hope or consolation. In this condition I was surprised by my servant, announcing a

stranger,

ſtranger, who earneſtly deſired to be admitted. The name of ſtranger awakened in me curioſity and expectation; I went out to meet him, and found myſelf in the arms of Sigiſmar. The affliction in which I was plunged gave way for a moment to joy and aſtoniſhment; but I was ſoon reminded of Valerius by the generous youth, who informed me, that he had purpoſely left Germany to communicate to me ſome circumſtances which he had diſcovered relative to the fate of my uncle; that, on his arrival at Rome, he had heard from Manfred I was departed for Campania, and by unwearied diligence he had traced me hither. I ſhould in vain attempt to deſcribe my ſurpriſe, or to tell the thanks which I expreſſed, and the anxious impatience with which I conjured him to loſe no time in relating all he had ſo unexpectedly learned: I could have fallen at his feet and worſhipped him as my guardian genius.

The

The excellent youth firſt acquainted me that he was reconciled to Arminius, who having diſcovered ſome new treachery of Philocles, had been induced to make enquiries into the conduct of the generous Cariovaldas, in conſequence of which he had reſtored his poſſeſſions to Sigiſmar. One day, while Sigiſmar was hunting with the chief, they found in a cavern three wretches, who by their habit appeared to be ſtrangers, emaciated with hunger, and almoſt lifeleſs with cold. Their ſtate excited compaſſion in the chiefs, and every means being uſed to revive them, they began to recover, and were found to ſpeak the Latin language. This excited ſtill more the pity of Sigiſmar, he enquired into their hiſtory, and received for anſwer that they were ſlaves, and had fled from their maſter, who was a Roman. He aſked them from what part they made their eſcape, to which they replied with the irreſolution and unwillingneſs of conſcious guilt.

guilt. Arminius fufpected they were fpies,
and would have put them to the torture; but
they were intimidated by the preparation, and
immediately confeffed that they had been
acceffary to the crimes of Sejanus, but not
concerned in any attempt againft the Germans.
This did not fatisfy Arminius; he repeated
his menaces, and they acknowledged that,
with two others of their companions, one of
whom was the director in their infamous
defign, they had been employed to convey
fecretly into exile a diftinguifhed and noble
fenator of Rome, whofe principles were of-
fenfive to the favourite; that in the fervice
of this fenator, they had experienced every
bleffing except liberty; but that enticed by
the promife of wealth and freedom, they had
acted in obedience to the command of Sejanus, whom they imagined to be interpreter
of the will of Tiberius; and having reported
at Rome the completion of their purpofe,
were fent to perifh in a remote part of the
Tauric

Tauric Cherſoneſus*. Being left to themſelves in this miſerable region, where their
two companions died of famine, they pene-
trated through the country, and with inexpreſſible difficulty and labour arrived at the
Danube, which they found frozen; and
croſſing it, they endeavoured to procure an
aſylum among the inhabitants of its borders,
but were conſtantly repulſed, becauſe their
neceſſity had ſometimes urged them to ſeize
the cattle on their way. Thus driven from place
to place, after innumerable hardſhips, they
wandered into the foreſt, where they were diſcovered by my friend and his commander. Arminius having heard their ſtory, ordered them to
immediate execution, but Sigiſmar interceded
for their lives, declaring that they had been
ſufficiently puniſhed by their powerful employers, for a crime which their ſervile condition naturally expoſed them to commit, if

* Crim Tartary.

E   it

it did not render them excusable. Arminius then interrogated them on the affairs of Rome, and the family of Marcus Flaminius: they immediately confessed that it was my uncle, whom they had been induced to betray in the following manner.

The flave under whose direction they acted, was a Syrian, named Rodias, who had long been employed to watch every action of Valerius; though, at the fame time, they acknowledged his intelligence could afford no fubject of complaint to Sejanus. They accompanied their mafter to Baiæ in the beginning of the former year, and Rodias, who was in conftant correfpondence with a freedman of the favourite, there heard from him the news of my return to the legions, and, at the fame time, received orders to intercept all letters which might arrive for Valerius: with thefe orders a plan was fent, which they were to purfue in confequence of a refolution then formed by Sejanus, to remove

my

my uncle from Italy, left, with the additional strength which my appearance would add to his party, some scheme might be formed to oppose the despotic measures of the emperor and his adherents. This plan was arranged with consummate artifice, and put in execution on the evening my uncle had fixed for his departure for Naples. As it was late when he sat out, his conductors pretended to mistake their way, and being armed, they secured the other slaves who refused to be accomplices in the crime. They travelled all night, and their injured master, finding all resistance vain, resigned himself calmly to his fate. During the day he was lodged in a house appointed by Sejanus, and they dispatched another of the servants, who was privy to the measure, with a feigned message from Valerius to give the false intelligence which I received from his freedman at Baiæ. The next night they pursued their way, observing the utmost secresy, and

E 2

arriving

arriving at Brundusium, conducted their prisoner to the dwelling of a person devoted to the interests of Sejanus, who industriously spread the report that Valerius had departed for Greece. A ship was prepared, when the noble exile and his lovely daughter were by night conducted on board. After first steering for Dyrrachium, the pilot changed his course and directed his vessel towards Sicily, where, sending off a boat to the commanding officer at Messana, they shewed an imperial order for permitting them to pass without delay or examination, being charged with a commission for Sardinia.

With these precautions they proceeded, and at length set their prisoners on shore at Ericusa, the most distant of the OEolian* islands, with only two attendants, one of whom was a female slave belonging to Valeria. All that came in the vessel were thrown into the sea except the five perpetra-

* OEolian islands, Isole di Lipari.

tors

tors of this atrocious deed; and thefe afterwards received from their employers in fome
meafure the punifhment they deferved.

The flaves affured Sigifmar that they had
often repented of the crime; but, being once
engaged in the fervice of Sejanus, they
could not retreat: they feemed to fee on one
hand riches and freedom, to reward their
fervices; and on the other, inevitable death
to fecure their filence.

Dreadful as this narration may appear,
it has yet freed my imagination from apprehenfion that the infidious enemies of Valerius
had put an end to his being. It is certain
that they were actuated by that pufillanimity
natural to corrupt minds, and took every
meafure to perfuade the public that his departure was voluntary; fearing that, if they
had deftroyed him, his death could not long
remain concealed or unpunifhed. They
imagined that a crime of fo black a die
would excite fuch remorfe in the perpetrators

as neither threats nor promiſes could wholly ſtifle; and to this fear I undoubtedly owe the preſervation of Valerius. It is probable they would not dare to embark on this ſide of Italy, as they could not have found a veſſel for their purpoſe without firſt acquainting Torquatus the commander in chief, whom they knew to be the intimate friend of Valerius. The intelligence of your Illyrian is now confirmed; but had he not perſonally recogniſed my uncle, it is likely he would have been deceived by the ſame account which was given to the officer at Meſſana.

To return to the gallant Sigiſmar, for whoſe fate I had ſo long been anxious, I know not how ſufficiently to acknowledge my ſenſe of his kindneſs.

"The ſecret," ſaid he, "appeared to me too important for epiſtolary communication, or for any ear but yours; my reaſon told me it was neceſſary to depart immediately for
Rome,

Rome, and my heart rejoiced at this opportunity of seeing my friend."

I conjured Sigifmar, as he was now thus happily reftored to me after fo long and painful an abfence, never to leave me more; and entreated him to accept of a villa, which I poffefs at Tibur, and which, though not fpacious, is enclofed by lands fufceptible of improvement, and fufficiently extenfive to fatisfy his defires. Sigifmar, however, perfifts in his intention of returning to Arminius, though from what I can collect by his filence on many particulars, rather than from his converfation, it appears that fince the defeat [*] of the Germans, who are now divided by inteftine difcord, Arminius feems [*] to have formed fome ambitious fchemes, which may end in an attempt to make himfelf the fovereign of Germany. Should this be true, the fentiments of Sigifmar are fo well known to

* Tacitus, Book 2.

E 4

me,

me, that I am affured he will never be acceffary to any defigns that tend to fubvert
the liberty of his country. The true fpirit of
patriotifm can alone detach him from Arminius, fince the injuftice which he has experienced from him has never prevailed upon
the virtuous Cherufcan to fwerve from his
fidelity. When I expreffed my indignation
at the protection granted to Philocles, and
the confequences that refulted from it, Sigifmar replied, " You muft confider, my
friend, that a prince and leader ought to ad-
minifter juftice impartially; and Arminius
could not, confiftent with his duty, have fuffered a kindnefs for me to lead him into a
blind belief of all I had related: you are not
ignorant of the plaufibility and talents of
Philocles; even you were once deceived by
him. Arminius attended to his declaration,
which, it muft be confeffed, had all but
truth to recommend it: he was fenfible of
the advantages he might reap from the
know-

knowledge and counsels of a man, who had seen and studied more than any individual of our nation. It was very natural Arminius should be deluded by his subtilty, but he has made ample amends by publicly declaring that my father was the friend of his country, and unjustly sacrificed. I never thought myself personally injured, but when he deprived me of the honour of being one of his companions. In this station he now offers to replace me, but I am doubtful whether I shall accept of it: the war is over, at least that which we waged against the enemies of our country: I have no desire for distinctions, when I can no longer deserve them: my reputation is independant of the favour of Arminius, though my attachment to him cannot end but with my life, or with his zeal for the real good of Germany."

LET-

I BROKE off abruptly, my dear Septimius, the laft time I was writing to you, as the wind fuddenly changed and favoured our departure for the Oeolian iflands. The fea, alas! has once more deceived my hopes: we were obliged to make for Lipare, and I can fcarcely flatter myfelf that the weather will allow me this evening to purfue my voyage to Ericufa. The delay diftracts me, and had it not been for the prudence of Sigifmar, who, in compliance with the entreaties of the mariners, prevailed on me to defift from my purpofe of braving the ftorm, we fhould perhaps have been driven out to fea by a tempeft which baffled all the fkill of our feamen. This generous youth is refolved

not

not to leave me till I have met Valerius; and his prefence is effentially ufeful to compofe my agitated mind.

You will readily conclude that I have not neglected an enquiry after Bertha and Vercennis Sigifmar is become the happy hufband of the former, though he frankly acknowledges that when he firft returned to his native plains, he found her immerfed in grief for my departure. He attributes his fuccefs to the efteem fhe conceived for him, in confequence of his friendfhip for Flaminius, and he imputed no blame to her for an unfortunate and innocent attachment. He fhared her forrows, and foothed them by his fympathetic attention, till his many amiable qualities at length met with the reward they deferved: his affection was returned, and the union of Sigifmar and Bertha forms the felicity of Vercennis, and they have an infant fon, born a few days before his departure for Rome. How great

muft

muſt be the ſenſibility of his friendſhip and the benevolence of his heart, that could influence him to forſake ſuch domeſtic ties, and ſeek a diſtant and hoſtile land, to inform me of the fate of Valerius!

On enquiring more nearly into the reaſons for which Philocles has been diſmiſſed from the ſociety of Arminius, I have learned that a clandeſtine correſpondence was diſcovered between him and ſome of the allied princes, who are either jealous of the power of the Cheruſcan leader, or fearful leſt their liberties ſhould be ſacrificed to his ambition. The Grecian is now with Maroboduus *, the chief enemy of Arminius : he is ſuppoſed to be the principal cauſe of the defection of Ingomar, who formerly abandoned the Romans to join his nephew, and now has left him, to court the favour of thoſe who are in oppoſition to his intereſt. It appears that Philocles has artfully inflamed

* Tacitus, Book 2.

the

the pride of Ingomar, and taught him to scorn obedience to a young commander, with whom he is so nearly connected. Such is the constant and treacherous duplicity of the Grecian, that men of this consummate depravity seem permitted to exist, that mankind may by experience be disgusted with artful plans and wily resources. From the repugnance I have always felt at the sight of a deserter, and the horror I have conceived for a wretch, who offers to betray the man in whose councils he once shared, I should think that none would ever confide in such characters. A secret impulse should impel us to shun them, even before we reflect that we may be the next victims of their artifice.

Nothing can be more awful than the appearance of this island*. As we approached, we contemplated the waves that reflected a

* The volcano of Lipare is mentioned by many ancient authors, and was not extinct till long after the date of these letters.

sanguine

fanguine colour from the fiery torrents that roll down the fide of the mountain. The moon, half concealed by clouds, appeared of a pale and fickly red; while the frequent explofions, accompanied by wreaths of fmoke, caft alternately on the tide a dazzling fplendor and a gloomy darknefs. As we came on fhore, the earth fhook under us, a fubterranean thunder rolled in the hollow cavities of the ifland, a rain of fulphureous ftones fell round us, or plunged hiffing into the fea. Sigifmar was not terrified, but he was ftruck with admiration and aftonifhment; and at length exclaimed—" Is this the beauteous Hefperia? Thanks to bounteous Nature! fhe has difpenfed her favours with a lefs partial hand than I once imagined!"

This is the only time I ever heard from Sigifmar an expreffion, which has not denoted univerfal benevolence, and could not help obferving it. " My friend," faid I,

" what

" what advantage could your countrymen reap from the confcioufnefs that, while they are expofed to the rigour of froft and fnow, the natives of this ifland are in danger of conflagration? The miferies of others can furely be no alleviation of their fufferings."

" Miftake me not," replied he with unufual warmth; " Heaven is my witnefs, I have no joy in difcovering the misfortunes of thefe regions; but I exult in every event that frees me from error or prejudice. I have always thought our brave Cherufcans were condemned by their fituation to peculiar hardfhips, while the fortunate Italian enjoyed uninterrupted bleffings: I have fometimes envied their advantages, not for myfelf, but for the wretches who toiled in our fields, or ftood motionlefs to guard our intrenchments. With the privileges you were fuppofed to poffefs, I could fcarcely confider you as our brethren; you appeared to me like beings exempted from the miferies

ries of human kind; I shall henceforth be more just, and my pity will be more exten- sive."

We strayed far into the interior part of the country, and found it wonderfully fer- tile, wherever the volcano has not lately extended its ravages. It is not possible to visit these islands without recalling to mind the fictions of the poets, which are mani- fest embellishments of physical as well as historical truths. With very little assistance from imagination, we may hear the resound- ing hammer of Vulcan, and the boiling of the metallic fluids, which are to compose the armour of the gods. When I observed in Sicily the gentle stream of Acis flowing from beneath a rock, which appears to have been flung by the hand of a giant, I traced the image back to its source, and was no longer surprised at the bold ideas which placed the Cyclops on these shores, and in- terpreted the tremendous force of inflam-

matory

matory matter as the jealous fury of an enraged minifter of the God of fire. Poetic wonders can thus be naturally explained; and I begin to find nothing wholly fictitious, except the fophiftry of pretended philofophers, and the fceptic reafonings of thofe who would deftroy fenfibility by phrafes, and make virtue dependent on felf-love.

We have paft the night in expectation of the tempeft abating; but the return of day has not cleared the profpect. The natives of this country are hardy, induftrious, and active; their features are regular, and full of expreffion; their figure manly and graceful. We have experienced great hofpitality from the principal citizens, of whom I enquired whether there remained any defcendents of the good Timafitheus*, who ruled their ifland at the time when our legates, being deputed to offer at the fhrine of Apollo the golden cup, vowed by Ca-

* Livy, Book 5.

F   millus

millus during the Veian war, and purchafed with the ornaments prefented by the Roman ladies, were taken by the pirates of Lipare, and fo generoufly fet at liberty by their governor. You have read that he not only lodged them at the public expenfe, but efcorted them with his fleet to Delphos, and afterwards reconducted them in fafety to Rome. His family is extinct; but the tablet, given by a decree of the fenate to entitle him to all the privileges of hofpitality, and the prefents which accompanied it, are carefully preferved by the Liparenfians in their public treafury. They were highly delighted at hearing that I was the fon of a Valeria; they knew that one of the family was at the head of this celebrated embaffy, and they earneftly requefted that I would take their ifland under my protection. I could not refufe to comply with the requeft, and was greatly affected to perceive their reverence for the Valerian name; whilft the beft and

nobleft

nobleſt Roman of that name, deprived of his honours, and ſecluded from human intercourſe, remained unremembered by that country which he defended, and oppreſſed by that prince whom he never injured.

LETTER

AT length, my friend, I have reached the hallowed ground where Valerius triumphs over the caprice of fortune, and the injuftice of man. At length I am reftored to his parental arms! What words can defcribe our meeting! What colours can paint the heroic firmnefs with which he ennobles misfortune!

It was late in the evening when we arrived at Ericufa; the winds were hufhed, and the tremulous light of the moon glittered on the furface of the water, while a few trees, fcattered along the coaft, intercepted its rays, and caft long fhadows on the plain. I fprung impatiently on fhore before our galley had touched it, and walked haftily towards a

light

light which appeared at a fmall diftance: Sigifmar followed me, and we difcovered that the light proceeded from the door of a hovel, to which we directed our fteps: we there found nets, lines, and other implements of fifhing: a woman, with a child fleeping befide her, was employed in fpinning, and feemed greatly aftonifhed at our appearance. We afked her to fhew us the way to the dwelling of Titus Valerius; fhe looked fteadfaftly on me for fome time without reply. I was alarmed, and repeated the requeft with agitation: fhe then faid, that fuch perfon was unknown to her; but that, if we were in diftrefs and wanted affiftance, there was, not far remote, a habitation, rather larger than hers, where dwelt a Roman with his daughter, who paffed their days in fuccouring the needy, vifiting the fick, inftructing the youth, and fettling the differences between the few inhabitants of the ifland. I wanted no further proof that

F this

this beneficent Roman muſt be Valerius.
I deſired that ſhe would accompany us
to the place; but ſhe ſaid that it was unneceſſary, as the path lay ſtrait before us,
and we could not miſtake our way. I waited
for nothing more, but rather flew than
walked towards the place to which ſhe
pointed, where I ſoon perceived a cottage ſurrounded with trees, and could ſcarcely believe that ſo humble a dwelling ſhould be
inhabited by one of the firſt of Rome's patricians—by a deſcendent of the Valerii. My
heart was full—I ſtood to compoſe myſelf,
and had not power to advance. Sigiſmar
felt for me: he preſſed my hand, and ſaid,
" Marcus! your uncle lives—how great
would be my tranſport if it were poſſible
that I could find Coriovaldas living, even in
the moſt miſerable cavern; but, alas! he is
gone for ever!—recollect yourſelf, my friend;
have you not often declared that true greatneſs

nefs does not confift in exterior circumftances ?"

"It is true, Sigifmar," anfwered I; "and
my heart tells me that I fhall find Valerius ftill
greater in yon cottage, than in the lofty
manfions where I laft embraced him."

This reflection, in fome meafure, reftoring
me to myfelf, I began to confider in what
manner I fhould difcover my arrival to my
uncle. Though I knew his mind fuperior
to the fhocks of misfortune, I was not certain but the fudden appearance of a beloved nephew, whom he honoured with parental affection, and whom he had long
lamented as flain, might produce an excefs
of joy and furprife that would fufpend his
faculties, and fhake that firmnefs which had
ever diftinguifhed his character.

As I was abforbed in thefe reflections,
and flowly moving towards the cottage, I
perceived a female figure dreffed in white,
feated under one of the trees; the moon

F 4

fhone

shone directly on the place, and the serenity
that was visible in her countenance, the
graceful majesty, and decent compofure of
her appearance, the radiancy of her eyes,
all convinced me it could be no other than
Valeria. You have feen her, my friend,
and it is needlefs to defcribe the impreffion
fhe made on me: we advanced rather too
abruptly; fhe was greatly alarmed, and
when we enquired for Valerius, fhe trembled
and turned pale, imagining we were come
with fome fatal order from Tiberius.. While
I was pierced to the foul at her miftaken
terrors, fhe fell on her knees, implored our
pity, and conjured us to fpare him. In
vain I attempted to fpeak—Sigifmar obferved my diforder, and informed her that I
was Marcus Flaminius, who had been faved
from the flaughter of Teutoburgium;
but it was fome time before fhe gave credit
to his words: at length, when fhe had
fufficiently recovered herfelf to turn her

eyes

eyes on me, she looked as if desirous to
trace in my features the truth of what she
had heard. " Speak to me," said she,
" assure me that you are Marcus." I know
not how I answered; you, my friend, will
conceive what must have been my agitation. Valeria then departed, with a signal for us
to remain in the same place: in a few minutes
she returned, and told me she had informed Valerius that a stranger was arrived
who could give him intelligence of his
nephew. She entreated me that Sigifmar
might first accompany her to Valerius, and
prepare him by a previous narrative to receive me. I consented; but no words can
give an adequate idea of my impatience. I
waited not long, before Valerius appeared, who
alarmed at the agitation of Valeria, and the
apparent confusion of Sigifmar, had rushed
forth to learn the cause: he ran to me, he
pressed me to his bosom—but I will not
wrong the scene by attempting to describe
it.

it. O Septimius! why were you not present to experience fenfations worthy your generous, your feeling breaft?

My uncle led me to his dwelling, where, as foon as I could collect myfelf, I prefented to him my friend, the fon of my benefactor. " This is the only time," exclaimed Valerius, " that I have regretted, from any perfonal motive, the loffes of fortune, and of my influence in the republic—How can I teftify my fenfe of the greateft of all obligations ?"

I looked round the humble habitation; Valerius fmiled. " Marcus," faid he, " Poplicola rendered more effential fervices to the ftate than I have ever had it in my power to do, and probably he was not more magnificently lodged."

It would be impoffible to give you an account of our evening's converfation; you may imagine that Valerius commanded me to relate every thing that had occurred to me fince

our

our parting.   His approbation of my conduct gives me a heartfelt fatisfaction beyond
all the pompous rewards I have received,
even beyond the acclamations of my country.
In him I venerate her majefly, united with
whatever is dear and refpected in nature.
Valeria appears to me the moft amiable
of her fex.

My tranfport is too great to allow me
repofe; and yet it cannot be complete
till I have communicated to Septimius the
reward of my long anxieties.   Though I
do not mean at prefent to difpatch any fervant from this ifland, I fhall continue to
write to the moft excellent of friends.

The morning appears, and I am impatient
to rejoin Valerius: how much have I to fay
to him! how much to learn!

LET-

THIS morning, as soon as the sun appeared above the horizon, I accompanied Valerius to the sea shore, where seating ourselves on a rock, he explained to me the causes which he imagined had excited against him the enmity of Sejanus.

" I have," said he, " always treated the favourite with indifference. While Tiberius was at Rhodes, I had an opportunity of being useful to some of his friends who deserved my assistance: at his return he shewed an inclination to form an intimacy with me, and his mother often hinted that she desired to hear my opinion on various subjects concerning the republic. I constantly replied, that I gave my opinion in the senate; at the

fame.

fame time I carefully avoided making any connexion with Livia or her fon; this you know, and may eafily fuppofe the reft. When the commonwealth loft Auguftus, I forefaw with regret that none but Tiberius would attempt to fill his place. It is true that a party might have been raifed againft him; but the event was uncertain, and the republic would have been expofed to all the horrors of a civil war, which muft fooner or later end in abfolute monarchy, whatever title the conqueror might affume. Germanicus, the only perfon of the Julian family whofe virtues made his government defirable, could not without a crime have difpoffeffed his adoptive father; nothing therefore remained for good citizens but to endeavour, as far as poffible, to curb the power of Tiberius, and to maintain the facred reliques of our rights and privileges.

" In former times, when luxury, the

chief

chief corrupter of mankind, was fcarcely known in our republic, ambition was di-rected towards the general good; or if any citizen, whofe abilities were greater than his integrity, attempted to form a party, his views were foon difcovered and defeated. As riches increafed, the partifans of men of diftinction grew into armies; the ftate was torn to pieces by the difcordant interefts of various leaders, each of whofe revenues were equal, perhaps fuperior to thofe of a powerful monarch, and whofe influence was confiderably more extenfive. Equality could no longer fubfift; and the chimerical idea which a few enthufiafts, rather than true friends to liberty conceived, that the ancient principles of government could be re-efta-blifhed in all their purity, when fimplicity and frugality were loft, only ferved to engage the powerful to ftrengthen their forces and increafe the means of feduction.   To put in force the Agrarian laws, when the moft

leading

leading men of the ftate are interefted in oppofing them, is certainly impracticable; and without an equal diftribution of the goods of fortune, or at leaft without preventing too great a difparity, no perfect commonwealth can fubfift. Brutus was perhaps one of thefe enthufiafts defcribed, and the conduct of his affociates is ftill lefs to be defended. It appears to me that Cæfar was neceffitated to act as he did; for had he fubmitted to the demands of his opponents and difmiffed his army, he muft have been the paffive affiftant in eftablifhing the fovereignty of Pompey. This was a part for which nature had not formed him: with the talents and virtues he poffeffed, had he lived in different times, he would have freed his country from the yoke of the Tarquins, he would have revenged on the Decemvirs the blood of Virginia, would have driven Hannibal out of Italy, and been fatisfied with the honours fpontaneoufly be-

ftowed

ftowed on him by his country: fuch was the conqueror of the Gauls, the pardoner of his enemies! Auguftus, by a long and peace-ful adminiftration, healed the wounds of civil difcord; few acts of injuftice were committed during his government, and internal peace diffufed profperity over our extenfive dominions. The Roman name was refpect-able throughout all nations, and the fhafts of misfortune feemed only directed againft the family of the ruler: we were as fortunate as the degeneracy of our manners could reafonably permit us to hope. Tiberius, notwithftanding his profound diffimulation, has already convinced us that he aims at more abfolute power than his predeceffor ever defired. We fhould repel every innovation of defpotifm, at the fame time that we preferve refpect for his perfon; remembering that our aged bark requires a pilot, though we muft not fuffer this pilot to tyrannize over the mariners, nor drive

the

the veffel on a rock.   Thefe are the maxims
which I have ever purfued, and which con-
ftituted the motives of my oppofition to the
dictates of Sejanus.   I was of opinion that
the fpirit of rivalry, among the heads of
the republic, which difappeared under the
fuperior power of Auguftus, might break
out afrefh, in a more dangerous and more
difgraceful manner, when fomented by an
infidious favourite for his illicit and felfifh
purpofes.   I wifh to revive the priftine zeal
of our nobles in defence of the laws of
Rome, and of the empire of Tiberius: I
can fcarcely believe that even the moft cruel,
avaricious, and lawlefs prince, unlefs im-
pelled by infatuation, can voluntarily feek
the ruin of his country, with the interefts
of which his own are fo nearly connected:
but narrow-minded minifters, who have
been raifed, without defert, to wealth and
power, who act merely for their private
ends, may calumniate the prince to his peo-
G   ple,

ple, and the nation to their fovereign; they may fpread corruption and diffention till they involve both in mutual calamities. I have no perfonal enmity to Sejanus, though I defpife his character, and fear, for the republic, the increafe of his influence; but I contented myfelf with repulfing the vanity that urged his pretenfion to the hand of Valeria. I never oppofed the promotion of any of his adherents to places by which the public fafety was not endangered; yet I am fenfible that my exile is owing to his artifices. I made no refiftance—the facrifice was not great to abandon a country where I muft have been hourly a fpectator of wrongs, which probably I fhould have in vain attempted to redrefs.

Whether fear or malice induced Sejanus to choofe for my retreat a neglected ifland, which has no communication with the continent; to place me in a habitation fcarce defended from the inclemency of the feafons, and to allow for my fubfiftance

only

only rocky ground, cultivated by two or three flaves, whom he, perhaps, commanded to watch my motions, but whom I have converted into ufeful and induftrious beings, all this, my dear Marcus, is totally indifferent to me; and fuch is the tendernefs of Valeria for her father, that fhe has acquired fufficient magnanimity to relinquifh, without a figh, the gay profpects that opened to her blooming years. I boaft of no ftoicifm; I love to enjoy and communicate the gifts of fortune; I regret my friends, and fometimes lament that I am ufelefs to my country; but I am confcious of having acted uprightly, of having done my duty; and neither defire of revenge, nor repining at deftiny, difturbs my repofe. One grief alone hung like a weight on my exiftence. Often in folitude and filence, the image of Marcus prefented itfelf to my imagination, and even that grief was ftilled, though not effaced, by my love for Rome, in whofe caufe you bled. What-

ever

is now my fate, Valeria will find in you
a friend and protector."

I was about to fpeak, but he prevented
me by proceeding; "I know, my fon, that
you would wifh to reftore me to my former
fituation; but fupplications would neither be
confiftent with your fpirit, nor with my
character. Thefe I am certain you would
difdain: every attempt to excite the minds
of the Romans againft their prince is ab-
horrent to my nature, and I would not
accept of liberty on fuch terms. Time may
change the face of affairs, and may give me
the means of returning with honour: in the
mean while I charge you, by your filial affection, and by the fervices you have done your
country, never to be led aftray by private
refentment. Reflect how many have become
guilty of irreparable crimes by engaging too
warmly in a caufe which was juft in the
beginning: I need not warn you never to be
feduced by a falfe ambition to court the

                                    favour

favour of any man, however powerful; or, when the laws of your country forbid, implicitly obey the dictates of any prince, even were he endowed with the virtues of a Germanicus. Believe me, Marcus, the best of men, when trusted with sovereignty, are liable to commit injustice, from the very benevolence and humanity of their dispositions. Strict impartiality in this world can only be found on tables of bronze, or of marble."

I represented to Valerius, that whatever might be his fate, I was determined to share it; that henceforth all my wishes centered in the desire of never being separated from him and Valeria, unless I could once more be so fortunate as to employ my arms in the service of my country; but that peace would be a stranger to my breast, while the injuries he received from Sejanus remained unpunished.

" Sejanus," resumed he, " had not power

to injure me; my fame, nay my happinefs,
has conftantly been independent of his malice; and the vain ftratagems he has employed deferve from Marcus no other punifhment than contempt. True greatnefs, my
fon, confifts no lefs in being fuperior to
perfecutions of this nature, than to the ills
they may have occafioned. I muft efteem a
man before I would refent his ill conduct.
Leave Sejanus to the certain, though perhaps
tardy, vengeance of the public, and think
only how you are to maintain, with unfhaken
dignity, the character of a Roman; when at
Rome, regardlefs of the infidious favours of
the great, and of the feditious applaufes of
the people; and when engaged in foreign
fervice, neither endangering the fafety of
your troops in the caufe of your private ambition, nor facrificing your laurels, and the
fplendor of our arms, to the fear of raifing jealoufy at home. But this exhortation is unneceffary; your warmth of difpofition and love
of

of glory require rather to be fuppreffed than excited; I charge you, therefore, to remember, that by ftrict moderation alone you can be effentially ferviceable to the republic. To her you muft dedicate your life: myfelf and Valeria are only to be fecondary confiderations; feclufion has not been my choice, but the circumftances which have led to it render it honourable, and not unpleafing to me. In you it would be criminal; you are deftined for an active life, and the difficulties under which Rome now labours, afford you an ample field for the exercife of every virtue; efpecially in thefe unfortunate times, when public degeneracy, more than the Cæfarean fortune, menaces Rome with flavery. There have been many proofs of heroic fortitude, of patriotic zeal, equal if not fuperior to what the moft fhining part of former annals can produce; and my prophetic hopes affure me that you will be con-

fpicuous

fpicuous with the brighteſt of theſe examples."

Our converſation was here interrupted by
the arrival of Valeria, and her preſence prevented my reply. She was welcomed by
her father with a ſentiment of pleaſure that
diffuſed a glow of cheerfulneſs over his
countenance.

Septimius, I have often formed in my
imagination an idea which ſeems realized in
Valeria. She has all the graces and inſtruction of poliſhed life, with the candour and
ſimplicity of the natives of uncorrupted
regions. The ingenuous Bertha ſometimes
appeared childiſh; the elegant Aurelia has
loſt her attractions in affectation, and perhaps there was always ſome mixture of artifice in her character, over which my partiality had caſt a veil; but never till now did
I truly experience that ſenſation which the
unfeeling calumniate, and the licentious pro-
fane. Do not accuſe me of haſtily giving

way

way to the first impreffion: all I had heard
of Valeria fince my return from captivity,
affured me that fhe was formed to make me
happy; and the fight of this lovely maid
has convinced me that I cannot be fo without her—but, alas! Septimius, I dare not
truft the rapturous profpect which my imagination would create. Valerius is infulted
and oppreffed; he will not allow me to fhare
his exile from the world; he has fhewn me
that it is incompatible with my duty; how
can I reftore him with honour to the fenate?
How can I prevail on him to confent to any
fteps that I may take to this effect? Should
I acquiefce with him in the heroic firmnefs
that makes him fubmit to his prefent fituation,
a fuppofition at which my nature revolts,
muft I difguife my thoughts whenever I
would wifh to vifit him? and when fhould
I not defire to fly to him for counfel, for
encouragment, in every virtuous refolution?
Could I bear to deprive him of the fociety

of

of Valeria, who sheds a balm over the cares of life; whose filial attachment compensates the lofs of every friend he once poffeffed? Would she confent to fuch a feparation? Nay, could I fupport the idea that I was living in felicity and fplendor, while my uncle, my protector, the moft diftinguifhed patrician of the republic, was plunged in neglect and indigence?

Thefe are thoughts that damp all the ecftacy I feel in being reunited to Valerius, and his too lovely daughter. Alas! my friend, are we to owe our mifery to the moft pleafing, the pureft, and moft natural affections of the foul?

LETTER

I AM made unfpeakably uneafy by a circumftance which, though inconfiderable in
itfelf, may be productive of fatal confequences. The Sicilian flave, who was recommended to me by Germanicus, made his
efcape three nights fince in the boat of the
poor fifherman, whofe hut we entered when
we firft difembarked on the ifland. He
compelled the owner to accompany him, as
we learned by the return of the fifherman
this morning, who feemed confufed and pe-
nitent: he confeffed that he had been terrified by the menaces of the flave, who came
to him during the night, accompanied by
another of my people, and forced him to
convey them to the ifland of Liparc. The
wife

wife was likewife conftrained to enter the boat with them, in order to prevent enquiry; and when we knew next morning of their departure, we had no means of purfuing them in time, my veffel being anchored off the oppofite coaft of Ericufa, where there is a fafer harbour. The fifherman, who never before made fo long a voyage, relates that the Sicilian flave had a veffel prepared at Lipare, in which he immediately fet fail for the continent, pretending that he was difpatched by me.

Valerius is willing to fuppofe that thefe flaves had no other motive for departure than the recovery of their liberty; but my anxiety is great, and from all circumftances I am convinced that we have every thing to fear for the fafety of my uncle, when once his enemies perceive that their villany is difcovered. I reproach myfelf for not having taken the neceffary precautions to prevent fuch a misfortune; but I find myfelf inca-

pable

pable of guarding against the complicated schemes of artful diffimulation. Were I the only victim, life would not be worth the attention requifite to inveftigate the plots of fuch men; but that my arrival fhould be fatal to Valerius! I cannot fupport the thought. O Septimius! fome artful means muft have been practifed to engage Germanicus to place this Sicilian in my family; and yet it might be imagined that this excellent prince, who is continually the object of treacherous enmity, would have miftrufted fome perfidy. I am certain that he could not intentially have deceived me.

Cariovaldas fpoke but too truly, when he faid that I fhould be condemned to a life of anxiety and perturbation. Amidft the wilds and deferts of Germany I was not furrounded by a race of beings ever ready to revolt by treachery againft the ftate of fubordination in which they live; yet it has been one of my conftant ftudies to make that ftate as

little

little felt as poſſible. Valerius laments with me that ſo large a portion of mankind ſhould, by ſervile occupations, loſe ſo much of the dignity of human nature, and that it becomes neceſſary to govern them with a ſtrict ſeverity, often more diſtreſſing to their rulers than to themſelves. "Inſtruction," ſays he, "and intellectual purſuits unfortunately cannot be general, and they whoſe minds are unenlightened, may eaſily be corrupted and ſeduced. Modeſt and induſtrious ſimplicity ſhould be the characteriſtic of the lower claſs of men; and we are in ſome meaſure to blame ourſelves, or rather the univerſal empire of luxury, for the crimes they commit, in conſequence of having been elevated to participate the pleaſures of fortune, without having enjoyed its only true advantage, that of a liberal education. Theſe reaſons induce me to overlook the treachery of Rodias and his companions, and ſhould lead you to pardon the Sicilian. The very ſituation in which

ſuch

such men are placed will habituate them to a perpetual concealment of their paffions and fentiments; and even thofe whom we inftruct in letters and fciences, are ftill obliged to live for us and not for themfelves."

In this manner does Valerius reafon on all the moral and cafual ills of life; his mind rifes fuperior to their power, and enjoys perpetual ferenity; like the fummit of fome lofty mountain unmoved by the ftorms, while the thunder rolls beneath, and the fable clouds involve the lower world in darknefs.

How far am I from having attained this exalted fortitude! and yet, Septimius, I am not anxious for myfelf. I intended to have paffed fome time in Ericufa; every thing attaches me to this fpot, and while I yielded to the inexpreffible tranfport of liftening to the engaging converfe of Valeria, and to the fublime philofophy of Titus, I found myfelf repaid for all my fufferings, and vainly hoped to fix in my unfettled mind fome plan for

my

my future conduct; but now every moment of my stay may increase the danger to which Valerius is exposed. I must tear myself hence to prevent the dreadful consequences which may arise from the slave's discovery: I must leave the objects of my tenderest affection, that I may not lose them for ever—the winds at present oppose my departure.

LET-

THE northerly wind, which has blown some days with peculiar violence, impedes all navigation, and lengthens the pain of parting: my heart is torn by contrary emotions, and nothing but my fears for the safety of Valerius could make me wish to leave this island. When my imagination presents to me the misfortune that may ensue from the least delay, I fly with impatience to the sea shore, in hopes that I shall perceive some change in the winds; and yet when I observe a cloud that seems to portend an alteration, my heart involuntarily forms a momentary wish that I may be still detained. Sigismar omits no opportunity of assisting and consoling me; to him alone I

H

dare

dare communicate the whole of my anxiety.
Valerius is undifmayed in the midft of
danger; and the facred awe impreffed on me
by the contemplation of his fortitude, for-
bids me to exprefs the leaft apprehenfion in
his prefence. Valeria has, in fome meafure,
loft her fears in the confidence of her father;
or, perhaps, fhe conceals them from the fame
motive. Heaven forbid that I fhould awaken
them! The ftudy of my life would be to
fhield her from the rude blaft of misfortune.
O! that I could prevent her ever knowing
forrow!

We pafs our days in the moft interefting
converfation, and every hour increafes my
admiration for Valerius. Speaking to him
of the vifit I had made to his villa at Baiæ,
and the demonftrations of affection to him
which I had witneffed in both the rich and
indigent inhabitants of the place, he turned
afide, and feemed to conceal a greater emotion than I ever faw before on his countenance,

tenance. He changed the difcourfe to his library, which, he faid, was the part of his poffeffions he the moft regretted. " While I had the advantage," continued he, " of confulting at pleafure the fage who could enlighten me with the experience of ages, I conceived that fuch communication was effential to my exiftence; and when public affairs, or the inevitable interruptions of fociety, kept me two or three days abfent from my filent preceptors, my imagination feemed languid, and my mind vacant. I am now accuftomed to be deprived of fuch refources, and feel the advantage from digefting more at leifure in my memory what I have formerly read;" nay," added he, turning to Si-gifmar, who liftens attentively to every word of Valerius, " when I confider the virtues, the judgment, the penetration and firmnefs in the charafter of your father, fuch as I am certain has been faithfully defcribed by Mar-cus, I begin almoft to entertain a doubt of the

H 2

útility

utility of books, and to suppose that curiosity, and the desire of knowing the thoughts
and actions of the wise and good, are the
principal incentives to reading : elegance of
style, and the various arts of persuasion,
which the study of eloquence imparts, are
other considerations. But though Cariovaldas wanted no assistance from the phi-
losopher, or the moralist, and practised
all, nay more than they have taught, without having consulted their works ; yet you,
Sigifmar, who have inherited his talents
and his virtues, you, who would be an ornament to any country, are commendable for
wishing to acquire the knowledge, which
a series of ages has diffused over this part
of the globe. It will give you advantages
which no wise man should contemn: it
will confirm you in the principles you have
adopted, and will convince you of the truth
never too often repeated, that wisdom and
virtue are but one."

Sigifmar

Sigifmar fhed tears at the mention of his father. "O Valerius," exclaimed he, "fince. I have loft Cariovaldas, why cannot I remain with you, and bring up his defcendants in imitation of his virtues and of yours."

I have been interrupted by the mariners, who inform me that the weather permits our departure. My troubled fpirits fcarce allow me to think—I muft not wait. Septimius! my friend! how can I bid farewell to Valerius and his daughter? The eaft reddens with the approach of day—I cannot depart without feeing them.

 LETTER

I WRITE to you, my friend, from on board my galley. Sigifmar repofes; our hardy rowers cut with meafured ftrokes the liquid element; the pilot fings at the helm; I alone am wretched; my perturbation increafes as I approach the fhores of Italy; in vain I look back at the clufter of iflands which are fcarce vifible on the horizon. What an immenfe fpace have a few hours interpofed between me and happinefs!

When I clofed my laft letter, in the utmoft agitation, I found Valeria rifen. She was walking flowly beneath the trees that fhade the dwelling: I faw her ftop, and, with eyes full of tears, contemplate the unfurled fails of my galley. When fhe perceived me, fhe thanked me for haftening my
departure,

departure, as she felt the necessity of my presence at Rome, and acknowledged that the flight of my slave had given her alarms, which she endeavoured to conceal before her father. Her filial affection, and-the confidence she placed in me, overcame all my resolution, or rather the little remains of fortitude, which I had attempted to collect, that I might be able to support the parting moment. Valerius found us in this situation; he embraced me; " My son," said he, " the only concern I have in this world, is the care of my honour, of Valeria, and yourself. I need not recommend to you the two first; but I charge you, by your love for me, by the tender and compassionate regard with which the unprotected state of my daughter inspires you, not to expose yourself rashly, nor to risk a life devoted to your country, in any service but that of Rome."

How can I obey him? What could I promise?

mife? 1 know not how I tore myfelf from his arms; long did I perceive him with Valeria on the beach; my eyes continued fixed to the fpot, while they could diftinguifh the beloved objects: even now, while I am writing, they turn involuntarily towards that part of the horizon.

A cloudy vapour has involved the neareft of the iflands—I am once more a folitary being in the wide univerfe—Why was I reftored to the protector of my youth, to the parent whom I have ever loved with inexpreffible fondnefs, and who is now more dear to me, far more dear, as the father of Valeria! Why did I enjoy a gleam of tranfitory rapture? Why has death fo often fled from my wifhes?

The excellent Sigifmar, whofe gentle and beneficent difpofition ever fympathifes with my fufferings, has given up one of the greateft of enjoyments, that of repofe and oblivion, to fhare the forrows of his friend. Septimius,

mius, you will pardon the wild expreſſions of my deſpair; the wretch whoſe heart is lacerated with poignant affliction, looks on ſleep and annihilation with longing eyes or with hopeleſs dejection.

I will rouſe myſelf from this exceſs of grief; my reſolution is ſettled, and whatever is the event, you ſhall be informed of it.

You will judge of the diſorder of my mind by the incoherence ſo apparent in my writing. I fly to you, the moſt valued of friends, for conſolation. Sometimes I ſtart, as from a deep reverie; and though every inſtant tranſports me further from Ericuſa, I impatiently enquire with what diſpatch we proceed on our voyage.

We are now at a ſmall diſtance from the Pontine iſlands, the place of baniſhment for many illuſtrious exiles, and particularly the wretched Julia: the ſight of them increaſes creafes my uneafinefs. Sigifmar, whofe mind is free from thofe ideas that cloud in my imagination, the beauteous appearance of nature in our once fortunate country, often ftands motionlefs with pleafure and admiration. The benefit of cultivation excites no lefs his attention, than the charms of nature: fully convinced of the advantages of agriculture, he regrets that the inftitutions of the Cherufcans are adverfe to this nobleft and moft harmlefs method of enriching a nation. The variegated fields of Campania attract his eyes far more than the fumptuous villas, whofe terraces project into the fea.

He is lately become acquainted with the immortal Æneid; and traces, with enthufiafm, every fpot celebrated by the poet. He would willingly have vifited the grotto of the Cumæan Sybil, and has learned, with delight, that Mifenum and Caïeta ftill retain the names given to them by the Trojan; but he is not dazzled by the fplendid embellifh-

ments

ments which Virgil has lavished on his hero.
He confiders him as an unjuft invader, who
robs Latinus of his power, and Turnus of
Lavinia; but is greatly interefted in the fate
of this unhappy prince, and juftifies the refentment of Amata. The only circumftance
which in fome meafure reconciles him to
Æneas, is his invariable piety towards An-
chifes. Had my mind been at eafe, I fhould
have received infinite fatisfaction from his
remarks, which flow fpontaneoufly from a
heart, uncorrupted by irregular paffion, fal-
lacious prejudice, or pernicious example.

LET.

WE met with a violent tempeft off the promontory of Circe *, and my impatience nearly caufed the deftruction of my friend, and of our gallant feamen: they perceived the ftorm increafing, and urged me to return to Caïeta; but unwilling to hazard any delay, I preft them to continue their courfe, vainly hoping we could reach Oftia; but finding this impracticable, I propofed we fhould make the port of Antium †. The feamen ufed all their efforts to obey me, and Sigifmar and myfelf gave what affiftance we could; but having paffed Aftura, the furge threw us on the coaft; the galley was fhat-

---

* Now called Mount Circello.

† Porto d'Anzio, a fmall fea-port in the Pope's dominions.

tered

tered into a thoufand pieces, many of our people were hurt, and hardly efcaped with life. This accident conftrains me to pafs a night at Antium, where we arrived on foot after great labour and fatigue. I have taken poffeffion of your villa *, and have experienced much attention from your fervants in fuccouring my poor feamen, whom I had almoft facrificed to my vehemence of temper.

I did not think it juft that Sigifmar fhould be deprived of the pleafure of vifiting fome of the wonders of art, with which the tafte and magnificence of latter ages have crowded this city and its environs. I conducted him to the gardens of Mecænas, and fhewed him the ftatue of Auguftus, placed by that minifter as prefiding over the tepid fountain, which he deftined to be, like that prince, for the

* The Septimii had a villa here; thofe of Mecænas, Atticus, Auguftus, &c. are taken notice of by feveral ancient authors.

good

good of the public. We then went to the elegant and simple dwelling of Pomponius Atticus, whose character I endeavoured to explain to my Cheruscan friend: for, at first, he did not seem inclined to think favourably of a man, who adhered to no decided opinion concerning the great events which determined the fate of his country; but when he heard that his universal kindness was not shewn during the prosperity, but in the adversity of each successive party or individual, he attributed his conduct rather to general benevolence, than to moral indifference or insensibility. To me it appears impossible to know Atticus, without esteeming and loving him; but at the same time, a man of his disposition may not unjustly be considered as a private benefit and a public evil.

We afterwards saw the pompous mansion of Tiberius, who has rendered this villa much more splendid than I remember to have seen it

when

when in the poffeffion of Auguftus. It was
here this great man received the beft of
titles; it was here that he was faluted
FATHER OF HIS COUNTRY: but the prefent
ftate of the apartments declares that they
rather belong to the mafter than the father.
A profufion of gold and precious ftones
appears in every room; the walls and pavement are of the moft coftly marbles, and
many ftatues have been added, amongft
which I obferved, with a mixture of admiration and difguft, a dying gladiator, in whom
the pangs of diffolution are expreffed with
fuch truth, as can only pleafe the artift, or
the tyrant. How different is the expreffion
of another ftatue in the fame portico! It reprefents a combatant fpringing forward to
attack an enemy on horfeback; ftrength and
agility are in every limb, courage and dignity
in the countenance, and with fuch animation
as might infufe fpirit into the coldeft bofom.
Sigifmar was delighted, but not aftonifhed

at

at the fight of this figure; the perfection of
art has fo much of nature, that he who is
unacquainted with the difficulty and pro-
greffive labour, by which fuch perfection is
attained, will not be furprifed at an excellence
which only correfponds with his own ideas
and obfervations.

We entered the temple of Fortune *, and
here I had an opportunity of obferving how
eafily my friend is induced to yield to reafon
and conviction. Having heard of this celebrated fane, and of its oracles delivered by
the drawing of lots, he was ftrongly tempted
to make the trial. I firft enquired of him
whether he really believed there exifted any
means by which it was poffible to obtain a knowledge of the future, except by
conjectures arifing from a combination of
paft incidents: he feemed doubtful, confeffed that he had never been firmly per-

* * Horace, Ode 36, Book 1.

fuaded of the gift of human prefcience, though few of his countrymen doubted of its truth, and the example of moft nations confirmed them in their opinion. He acquiefced in my arguments againft the benefit of forefeeing events, and confented to relinquifh his firft intentions, defiring to hear my opinion of the empire of Fortune in general. I reprefented to him the evident inconfiftency of fuch belief in her power: "If Fortune," faid I, "diftributed good and ill amongft the inhabitants of the earth, and the univerfe were governed by chance, our prayers would be of little avail to fo capricious a Divinity, whofe very name implies irregular cafualty; but if, as we have every reafon to fuppofe, an all-powerful, juft, and merciful Being watches over us, and difpenfes bleffings and misfortunes, according to his wifdom and our deferts, it is to him we fhould direct our fupplications, or rather, it

is

I

is in him we should place our trust. The
rest is superstitious error and idle curiosity:
whatever events are to happen, it is our
duty to meet them with intrepidity ; and we
could do no more, if by foreknowledge we
were prepared for them."

Sigismar blushed, and confessed that soli-
citude for the future was generally incon-
sistent with true fortitude: he willingly
quitted the temple, and we passed near the
ruined monument erected to the memory of
Coriolanus by the Volscians, after murdering
him for his tardy repentance of the injuries
he had done his country. Sigismar contemplated the decayed structure with pecu-
-liar attention, and then turning to me, asked
what we Romans thought of the man whose
ashes lay there entombed. I answered, that
we neither loved him as a friend, nor
esteemed him as an enemy ; that his resentment had corrupted his principles, and that

his

his former virtues were effaced by the greatest
of all crimes.   Sigifmar heaved a deep figh,
and preffing my hand, "Marcus!" faid he,
"the Romans are not the only men, who
have a country, and who muft not join her
enemies."

It was now late, and we returned to your
villa, where I met thofe of our mariners
who had leaft fuffered, and who had ftopped
on our way at the Temple of Neptune* to
fufpend at the fhrine fome reliques of our
fhipwreck.   The fhores re-echoed with their
acclamations, and they were impatient to
tempt once more the faithlefs element, in a
bark which your people had provided.   But
as there is no expectation that the fea will
permit our departure this evening or to-morrow, I fhall continue my journey to Rome
by land, and mean to fet out at break of

---

* In this place is a fmall town and fortrefs, with a
palace, Pomfili, belonging to Prince Doria.

day. Farewell, Septimius, your servants have taken the charge of dispatching my letters to you—my next will inform you whether we are slaves or Romans.

SEPTIMIUS, I never concealed my intentions from you till in my laſt two letters. Accuſtomed to open all my heart to my friend, this concealment has given me uneaſineſs; and nothing but the fear of involving you in that ruin, which ſeemed to hang over our family, could have reduced me to ſuch painful neceſſity.

I arrived at Rome early in the afternoon, and immediately went to the palace. The commander of the Prætorian guard, who was on duty, informed me the emperor had given orders that none ſhould be admitted: I anſwered that the honour and ſafety of Tiberius were concerned in what I had to ſay; the officer perceived I was determined, and

ſuffered

fuffered me to pafs. In the antichamber I found the ufual crowd of freedmen and flaves of all denominations, who are fuffered to enter while men of rank and independent citizens are excluded. I applied for immediate audience and obtained it, when Tiberius had been acquainted with the urgency of my requeft: he received me with a countenance on which appeared a kind of fmile, and commanded that we fhould be left to ourfelves. I thus began:

" A Roman patrician, who has ever done his duty to his country, in the moft diftinguifhed manner, both in the field and fenate, has been forcibly conveyed by his own flaves to a remote ifland, where he has been left near two years, in a ftate unworthy of the meaneft of his dependants. He has been torn from his honours, his poffeffions, and his friends: three of thefe flaves yet furvive, and accufe a more powerful, and more complicated villain,

of

of being the firſt inſtigator of their crime, while this villain ſhields his guilt under the ſacred name of Tiberius. Your honour is more intereſted than that of Valerius in clearing up this infamous tranſaction, and in reſtoring him to his former dignity: your ſafety is dependent on his."——

I expected to have found Tiberius embarraſſed: he was calm, and I proceeded.

" Valerius has convinced me that in its preſent ſtate of degeneracy, a chief is neceſſary to our republic: the unſhaken love which he bears his country attaches him firmly to the man, whom the will of Providence, and no mean talents of his own, have placed in the higheſt ſtation which can be filled by a mortal. He venerates in you the majeſty of Rome, and would defend your life as he would guard the capitol; but he may fall a victim to the treacherous deſigns of thoſe, who are enemies to the ſtate, and incapable of regard for Tiberius: with him

may

may vanish all remaining loyalty to a prince who once declared he only accepted of sovereign power that he might be useful to his country. Valerius may perish—and Marcus Flaminius will not survive his death, because he cannot revenge it without disobeying his paternal injunctions. But the Roman fire is not extinct; it animates the breast of many heroes whose intrepid valour will crush the hydra of insidious politics, and with the tremendous arm of justice annihilate the murderers of the great descendant of Poplicola."

Tiberius changed colour, but his features were scarcely discomposed, and he soon wholly resumed the emperor.

"Marcus," said he, "I commend, and thank you for your zeal; I have already informed you of my sentiments in favour of Titus Valerius; you are not rashly to credit the testimony of a few guilty slaves, who seek to calumniate others as an excuse for

their

their crime; neverthelefs enquiries fhall be made, and due punifhment inflicted on the guilty; in the mean time you will find that the principal caufe of your complaint has been removed. I no fooner learned from my fon, that the retreat of Valerius was involuntary, than I reprefented the affair to a fenate, which I convoked on the occafion; I entreated the confcript fathers to depute two of their moft honourable colleagues, Valerius Maximus and Meffala Corvinus *, to conduct your uncle back to Rome. Four days are elapfed fince their departure: they have taken the road of Putcoli, and are by this time embarked for the ifland of Ericufa, as I gave orders that Torquatus fhould fupply them with veffels. If the wind is favourable, you may fhortly expect to fee Valerius and his daughter; and I hope you will for the future be lefs rafh in your fufpicions,

* The Maximi and Corvini were branches of the Valerian family.

and

and lefs precipitate in your proceedings. My efteem for your uncle, my confideration of your fervices, and the defire I entertain of being more nearly connected with men who prefer the good of their country to every other confideration, all engage me to banifh from my remembrance the hafty and reprehenfible manner in which you firft addreffed me."

I was ftruck mute with aftonifhment, my dear Septimius, but, I confefs, did not yield an implicit belief to the information that was given me; at leaft I conceived there muft be fome artifice concealed in a meafure that feemed too generous for the difpofition of Tiberius. Notwithftanding his cenfure of my temerity, I fhould have ventured at fome interrogations, had I not been prevented by the entrance of feveral perfons, who had waited for an audience, and whom the emperor ordered to appear as foon as he had anfwered me.

I imme-

I immediately went to Germanicus, who, happily for my peace of mind, is not yet departed for Syria. He received me with inexpreffible pleafure, felicitated me on the fpeedy return of Valerius; and removed all my doubts for the prefent, by affuring me that the deputation had been publicly fent, and that Drufus was the perfon who had perfuaded the emperor to a meafure fo contrary to what might have been expected from the known influence of Sejanus, and the ftrong fufpicions that appeared againft him.

My fatisfaction is not complete, and I made no fcruple of avowing to Germanicus, that however fenfible I might be of the friendfhip of Drufus, I could not difguife my difapprobation of the means by which he muft have acquired his information of the place to which Valerius had been banifhed.

Germanicus feemed tacitly to agree with me, and lamented that I fhould have reafon to complain of the Sicilian, whom he had

recom-

recommended: he recollected that Drufus had often employed him in commiffions of little confequence, and praifed his intelligence; but he convinced me clearly that he was far from approving the ftep, which his brother had taken on this occafion, though he believed it to proceed from the zeal of friendfhip.

My firft idea was to fet out immediately for Campania in hopes of meeting Valerius, but Germanicus affures me that he is to be conducted by fea to Oftia: I muft therefore wait with refignation, but it is impoffible to defcribe what I feel.

I wifhed impatiently to have an explanation with Drufus; but, much to my mortification, I learned that he was gone on a hunting party into Sabina, and would be feveral days abfent. His conduct difpleafes me greatly; it might have been productive of the moft fatal confequences, and I fear the motive is not merely generofity or friendfhip.

Forgive

Forgive me, Septimius, if I judge too hardly of your friend; I have no conception that noble actions are to be pursued by clandestine means; truth and honour love the day. My obligations to Drusus will embarrass me; for how can I be grateful when I disapprove of his proceeding, and yet how can I resent a measure that restores Valerius to dignity and peace?

LETTER

TO my former uneafinefs, which, however abfurd it may appear, is beyond my
power to remove, may be added the pain
I feel for Sigifmar, who has not received any
accounts of Bertha, or of his family, though
he had given them inftruuctions in what manner intelligence might be conveyed to him
at Rome. They only are acquainted with
the place to which his journey was directed,
and even to them he did not communicate
the motive of his fudden departure. At my
return home laft night I found him leaning
againft the pedeftal which fupports a buft of
the unfortunate Demetrius *. You know

* Son of Philip, king of Macedon, brought as an hoft-
age to Rome by Titus Flaminius, and much beloved
there. Livy, Book 33.

with

with what tender regard we have always preferved this image of that too amiable prince, who was the victim of his attachment to the Romans, and of the malignant jealoufy of an unworthy brother. Sigifmar had learned his ftory, and was greatly affected by it. "Unhappy youth," faid he, "what muft have been his feelings, when he was forced to leave this hofpitable roof, and return to a country where, divided between the ties of nature and gratitude, he muft either become hateful to his neareft connexions, or forgetful of his generous benefactors, with whom he died in the attempt to reconcile thefe oppofite duties. Oh! my friend, how painful it is to renounce a happinefs which fprings from the pureft fource! How often muft Demetrius have looked back to thefe facred walls! How often, amidft the fnares and perfecutions which furrounded him, muft he have called on the name of Quintius Flaminius, and fupplicated the Gods to

shower

shower down blessings on the beloved mansion which he was doomed never more to behold!"

Sigismar burst into tears as he pronounced these words, and soon after acquainted me with his intention of immediately returning into Germany. He leaves me to-morrow, and I cannot but reflect on the regret which I shall feel in bidding him farewell; but his distress is great, and I dare not detain him any longer.

I have received a letter from Drusus, in which he endeavours to excuse himself for having made use of my attendant to learn that I had discovered the retreat of Valerius. He urges the necessity there was for an immediate application to the emperor, before Sejanus could have any knowledge of the circumstance; and adds that, when he returns, he will explain more fully his reasons; and, in the mean time, so earnestly entreats my forgiveness, with such apparent sincerity, as clearly evinces how much he is interefted for the family of Valerius.   Oh Septimius! never was I more perplexed: Drufus is the laft man in Rome to whom I would have owed this obligation: it wounds me more than you can poffibly conceive.

I have here found feveral of your letters, and thank you moft fincerely for the kind folicitude with which they are written.   I fometimes painfully reflect on the conftant difquietude which I communicate to you: my life has hitherto been a feries of troubles, and they have obliged me to break through a maxim which I had adopted at a very early period of life, never to diftrefs my friends by making them fharers of my grief. It is, perhaps, the moft pardonable fpecies of egotifm, but ftill it bears the character of that difgufting weaknefs.   A friendfhip, lefs generous and lefs conftant than yours, would not fo long have heard, with complacency, a fucceffion of complaints; but had I not been

without

without anxiety on your account, I fhould not have filled my letters with my own afflictions. Thank heaven! the virtues of my friend have been exempted from fuch trials! May no reverfe in his fortune ever call from me a proof how deeply I fhould feel his forrows. It is true, Septimius, that I could excufe myfelf by faying that not my own, but the calamities of thofe deareft to my heart have dictated my querulous epiftles— yet are not thofe friends fuperior to misfortune, and is it not for my own fake that I am afflicted? Alas! I cannot feparate myfelf from thofe I love : I exift only in them : all I have muft be devoted to them, except my honour; and without that, I fhould not be worthy of their regard.

I am concerned to find that Germanicus * is going on the Syrian expedition without a friend in power whom he can truft; even

* Tacitus, Book 2.

Syllanus,

Syllanus, who is allied to him, feems pur-
pofely removed to make way for Pifo, who
has inherited a fettled hatred for the Cæfarian family from his father, who oppofed
Julius in Africa, and afterwards followed
Brutus and Caffius. The fon has that dark
and malignant difpofition, which is always
inimical to the fortunate, and affumes the
mafk of difintereftednefs and independence,
to conceal jealoufy and envy. His wife Pla-
cina, powerful from her riches and connexions, is too much a flatterer of Augufta
not to be the enemy of Agrippina; and I
forefee that all the plans of Germanicus will
be counteracted, and all his intentions mif-
reprefented. He fees but too clearly the
defigns of his enemies, yet continues inflex-
ible in his refolution to obey the voice of
duty.

I introduced Sigifmar to him this morning, and nothing can exceed the demonftrations of efteem with which he received him.

                      Soon

Soon after our entrance we were furprifed with the voice of repeated acclamations *, and, on enquiry, found it proceeded from the Palatine library, where the lovers of literature were affembled to hear a new poetical compofition. Germanicus propofed that we fhould increafe the number of auditors, as Sigifmar expreffed the greateft curiofity to be prefent at a meeting of this nature. He was ftruck with the magnificence of the portico, and the ftatues of the Belides †, placed alternately between the columns. The crowd was immenfe, and Germanicus repented of his propofal, when he difcovered that the poet was celebrating his victories on the banks of the Vifurgis. He is naturally averfe to hear his own praifes, and his delicacy was alarmed left any expreffion might

* Pliny, Epiftle 13. Book 1. fpeaking of the emperor Claudius.

† Ovid, Propertius, &c.

wound

wound my Cheruscan friend: however, he considered that, by withdrawing himself abruptly, he would disturb the assembly, and mortify the poet; but, happily, this last had sufficient judgment to avoid in his composition those reflections on a vanquished enemy, which are not only illiberal in themselves, but injurious to the glory of the conqueror. The grammarian Apion*, who was present, joined warmly in the vociferous applause; but took notice, to those who stood round him, of many words and sentences which he condemned as improper, or negligent. Germanicus was displeased at a liberty which appeared to him injudicious, as it could not be authorised by critical knowledge. Apion, an Egyptian, can hardly be a competent judge of the elegance of our language; and I was myself disgusted at his censures, which were trivial and pe-

* Aulus Gellius, &c.

K 3   dantic;

dantic, but I could not help remarking to
Cæsar, that such were the natural confequences of thefe affemblies. When Afinius
Pollio * introduced the cuftom of reading
literary performances in public, he gratified
his own vanity, which feems to have been
exceffive; but experience muft have convinced us, that he rendered little fervice to the
learned world. Before thefe eftablifhments
were known, we had far greater poets than
we can now boaft. Virgil, Horace, and
Varius, read their works to a few felect
friends, whofe candour and judgment were
unqueftionable; they availed themfelves of
their criticifm, and were not vain of their
approbation. Though Pollio was amongft
the number of their learned protectors, we
know that they difapproved of his ideas in
this refpect, and forefaw the effects of them.

* Arfinius Pollio introduced the cuftom. Seneca,
Controv.

Our

Our prefent men of letters are applauded in public, and ridiculed in private. Mifled by the acclamations, which they interpret as the voice of fincere approbation; they do not reflect that fuch literary meetings are too numerous to be inftructive, and that felf-confidence is the only quality which they tend to infpire. After the poem was ended, Germanicus conducted Sigifmar through the library, and fhewed him the innumerable volumes that compofe this interefting collection; a gift worthy of Auguftus to the Roman people. The Cherufcan was aftonifhed at the fplendid appearance of the temple of Apollo, and the majeftic beauty of the Pythian Divinity *; the graceful attitude, the flowing drapery, and the air of poetic infpiration, with which

---

* Ovid, &c. A ftatue in this attitude, and with fimilar drapery, is to be feen at the Mufeum Pio Clementino, and has a Marfyas on the lyre.

K 4

he

he ftrikes the lyre, made a fingular impreffion on my friend. He obferved on the
harp a fmall figure of Marfyas, in baffo-
relief, and afked me why fo great an artift,
as Scopas *, fhould have fingled out the
moft unworthy triumph of Apollo for the
decoration of fo excellent a performance. I
endeavoured to account for it as an emblem
of fevere juftice, and as a warning againft
prefumptuous vanity; and it is highly probable that fome reafon of this fort induced
our anceftors to place, at the entrance of the
Forum, a ftatue of the fame Marfyas†,
which difgufts me whenever I pafs that
way.

Sigifmar was pleafed when we informed
him that the fumptuous luftre‡, reprefenting
a tree loaded with brilliant fruit, was taken

* Pliny the Elder.
† Horace, and others,
‡ Pliny,

by

by Alexander the Great at the fiege of Thebes,
and by him confecrated in a fane of the
fame Deity, to whom Auguftus again dedicated it. We fhewed him the place where
the Sybilline books were depofited, the
ivory doors, and other objects of curiofity,
which attract the eyes of a ftranger. Germanicus then led him into a large hall,
which he defired him to obferve with particular attention. "This place," faid he,
"once belonged to a man who fell with
diftinguifhed bravery in an unjuft caufe.
This was part of the houfe of Catiline,
fince united to the Cæfarian habitation, and
deftined by Auguftus for the nobleft purpofe.
He had appointed Verrius Flaccus* to be the
preceptor of his adoptive fons, Caius and
Lucius; and as this learned and virtuous
would not abandon the other youths whom
he had undertaken to educate, Auguftus

* See his life amongft the Grammarians.

removed

removed the master and his numerous scholars into this palace, giving them this hall for their literary studies. His sons were thus brought up with emulation and patriotism in the midst of their fellow citizens, whilst he presided over their studies, and himself instructed them in the use of arms, and other manly exercises. In this school was laid the basis of that education which rendered my father Drusus one of the greatest and best of men, and consequently to this I owe the inestimable advantage of his precepts and example."

As Germanicus was speaking, the respectable Verrius, who still inhabits the contiguous apartments, and preserves all the faculties of his mind at a very advanced age, walked through the hall leaning on the arm of two senators,. who had formerly been his pupils. Germanicus accosted him with affectionate respect, and I was delighted that my friend should be witness of an

incident

incident that proves we are not totally degene-
rate. He saw the reverence paid to an aged and
unambitious man, to the son of a freedman,
whose talents were never employed to render
himself illuftrious, but to form honourable
leaders, wife ftatefmen, and ufeful citizens
for the commonwealth; who was contented
that labour fhould be his portion, whilft
fame was that of his fcholars; defiring no
other reward than the fuccefs of his inftructions; and who confecrated to the public
good the juft munificence of a prince, whofe
greateft merit was the power of diftinguifh-
ing merit in others.

Sigifmar was not infenfible to the fcene
before him, and you will readily believe
that he was tranfported with the manners and
converfation of Germanicus.

" I am not furprifed," faid he to me, as we
were leaving the palace, " at the many examples I have read in your hiftory of marks
of regard received by your generals from the
enemies

enemies againſt whom they had fought. The Sicilians who choſe Marcellus for their patron, the Macedonians and Spaniards who carried the bier of Paulus Emilius, and the various nations that wept over the funeral pyre of Julius Cæſar, paid only a due tribute to the generoſity and benevolence with which they had been treated : in this I cannot but confeſs you ſuperior to the reſt of mankind."

In our way home, I conducted my friend through the Forums * of Auguſtus and Cæſar; in the firſt I pointed out to him the principal heroes of our republic, and in the ſecond I ſhewed him the equeſtrian ſtatue of the man in whoſe perſon were united the talents, generoſity, and valour of them all. Alas! why is perpetual dictator inſcribed on the pedeſtal !

* A full deſcription of them in Nardini, taken from ancient authors.

A SINGULAR event detains Sigifmar, and affords me the fatisfaction of being ufeful to him. It had been reported for feveral days at Rome that legates were on their way from Germany, difpatched by Maroboduus and Ingomar; but the time of their arrival was uncertain, and it was by the greateft chance imaginable that my friend did not leave the city, without knowing how much he was interefted in their embaffy.

Yefterday, when I had finifhed writing, I reflected that he had not been at the field of Mars, and I accompanied him thither early in the afternoon.

After fhewing him the elegant theatre of

Marcellus

Marcellus*, the temple of Bellona†, and the column from which our confuls throw the javelin as a declaration of war. I led him to the circus built by Caius Flaminius, whofe memory I refpect as much as that of my more fortunate anceftors, notwithftanding his contempt of omens, and his more ferious defect of imprudent temerity. When a general dies bravely defending the lives of thofe committed to his care, and fuftaining with his laft breath the honour of his country, the inaufpicious name of Thrafymene fhould not deprive him of the homage due to his virtues from his defcendants.

My friend had not time to fee the gardens and lake of Agrippa, the theatre of Pompey, nor the portico and grove where the young

---

* Palazzo Savilli, belonging to the Orfini family: a great part of the ancient edifice remains entire.

† See Nardini. For the buildings of the Campus Martius, and the beauty of the place, fee Strabo, Nardini, &c.

and

and thoughtless loiter away those hours which would be better employed in attending more diligently to the exercises of the field of Mars. Why these reflections? cries Septimius, have we not often wandered together amidst these scenes, and has not Marcus been the most unwilling to leave the walks of plane trees, notwithstanding his passion for the field? Would he not probably still frequent them, if his honour and his inclinations were not more warmly engaged in nobler pursuits? I confess it, my valued friend; the present agitation of my mind renders me inattentive to many objects that formerly attracted my notice, or at least they now strike me in a different manner. I rather recall to my imagination the events to which they owe their celebrity, than feel any astonishment at the sight of the various beauties, with which art and nature have adorned these meadows, interspersed with temples, monuments, and villas.

I pointed

I pointed out to Sigifmar the tombs of Hirtius and Panfa; and that of Julia, daughter of Cæfar, one of the moſt amiable, and furely one of the moſt unfortunate women, if the dead have any knowledge of the actions of their defcendants.

The maufoleum of Auguſtus* peculiarly affected me; I was perfonally attached to him, and all that is related of his grief for the deſtruction of our army has endeared him to me more than ever. The charms of his converfation, the pleafing dignity and intelligent penetration that ſhone in his afpect, returned to my remberance, and I could not avoid reflecting with horror on the early fate of all, except Germanicus, who ſhared his parental regard.—May the immortal Ruler of the univerfe long preferve the laſt from the baleful ſhade of thefe imperial cypreffes!

* The remains of the maufoleum of Auguſtus are to be feen in the garden of Palazzo Correa: they ferve as a theatre for bull-fights, fire-works, &c.

Hence

Hence I conducted Sigifmar to the temple of Neptune, and the fplendid portico of the Argonauts*. Amongft the ftructures raifed by Agrippa, there is none which, in my opinion, merits greater praife for the elegance of the columns, the beauty of the paintings, and the general magnificence of the ornaments, fo well adapted to perpetuate the remembrance of his naval victories.

On our return we paffed by the public villa, and while Ia cquainted my Cherufcan friend that it was the habitation allotted for ambaffadors, we perceived fome Germans ftanding round the gate. Curiofity prompted us to afk if the legates were arrived, when we received for anfwer, that they were hourly expected; and to our great aftonifhment we learned that they had brought with them the traiterous Philocles. This roufed the indignation of Sigifmar, and excited the

* The columns and frife of the cuftom-houfe in Piazza di Pietra, are fuppofed to have been part of this portico.

VOL. II.Lfame

fame emotion in your friend. I immediately
requefted Germanicus to acquaint the emperor
with the crimes of which the Greek had
been guilty, that he might be on his guard
againft a man with whom no negotiation
could be fafely conducted. But how much
were our furprife and refentment increafed,
when we difcovered that, among the hoftages
who accompanied the legates for pledges of
the fincerity of the princes, Ingomar had
fent the amiable Bertha as one of his neareft
relations ; and Vercennis, who would not
abandon the wife of her fon, has with his
infant accompanied the embaffy. Such proceeding is wholly unjuftifiable on the part of
Ingomar: for fince the marriage of Bertha
with Sigifmar, her family has no right to
difpofe of her, and his abfence alone has
given them an opportunity of ufurping to
themfelves fo unlawful a power.

In the firft tranfport of his joy, Sigifmar
forgot the affront that had been offered him

in

in the perfon of his wife: he flew to embrace Vercennis, and Bertha, and when he returned to me, feemed agitated by a mingled emotion of pleafure and refentment. I have this morning reprefented to our rulers the injuftice of this tranfaction, demanding that the family of Sigifmar fhould be exempted from the general laws relative to hoftages; and have provifionally obtained that they fhall be permitted to refide with him in my villa at Tibur, which one of my freedmen has been fent to prepare for their reception; and to-morrow Sigifmar will conduct them thither. The place is more congenial to his difpofition than the pomp and tumult of Rome; and the principal motive for removing Vercennis and Bertha from the perfons with whom they came, is to take them from the power of Philocles. This traiterous Greek carefully avoids to meet Sigifmar; and I am perfuaded his defigns muft be very deeply laid, or he would not have ventured

to Rome at the hazard of finding me, and
many others who are not unacquainted with
his former life, and particularly with the
fecret intelligence which he kept up in the
camp of Germanicus to the detriment of the
Roman interefts.   The character of legate
renders, for the prefent, his perfon inviolable,
and he is too well inured to guilt to blufh at
detection.

The caufe of this embaffy is faid to be the
defeat of Maroboduus * by Arminius, who
attacked him in a pitched battle, and, with
his ufual bravery, compelled him to fly into
the territories of the Marcomanians †.   Deferted by many of his troops and allies, Maroboduus implores the affiftance of Rome
againft Arminius, whom he ftiles the common enemy.   The motive of this legation
opens a new fource of difquiet to Sigifmar :
attached firmly to his prince, he cannot fup-

* Tacitus, Book ii.   † Bohemians, &c.

port

port the thought that his family fhould have been involved in fuch a meafure, and deplores the fate of his country, expofed to all the deftructive confequences of a civil war, excited by the ambition and enmity of its moft powerful fovereigns.   He ftill believes that Arminius is willing to defend the liberty of Germany, for which he firft took up arms; but appears to doubt whether the ftruggles of thofe who envy his fucceffes, and oppofe his paffion for fame, may not at length urge him to affert his power by acts of defpotifm.   He has written to the leader to clear the innocence of his family, compelled by Ingomar to join the embaffy, and has requefted his counfel in what manner to act in fo delicate a fituation.

The folicitude for my friend has, in fome fort, employed my time and attention; yet the three days which I have paffed at Rome, fince my return from Ericufa, have appeared to me of immeafurable length, but a much

L 3

longer

longer period must elapse before I can hope for the arrival of Valerius. My thoughts revert every instant to the happy hours that were spent with him and Valeria, while the images arising from such reflections supplant all other objects which once afforded me delight. Such is the painful effect of absence from those we love: it robs nature of every interesting charm, and art and science of every grace and utility; it destroys the efficacy of those resources which we should otherwise employ to cheer our solitude, because it usurps the empire of our mind, and leaves us scarce any attention to bestow on the common pursuits of life.

LETTER

SIGISMAR is gone with his family to Tibur, furrounded by the perfons who are moſt dear to him, and enjoys that ferenity which, though denied to me, I rejoice to contemplate in another.

It has been my endeavour to obferve your injunctions, and to divert my thoughts from gloomy images, by an attention to works that ſpeak at once to the heart and the imagination; and though this can at moſt be only a temporary relief, yet never will I neglect the counfels of my friend.

I have been to vifit the painter Lyſias, whom I employed, when I firſt arrived from Germany, to compofe two hiſtorical pieces, which I intend as a prefent for the vener-

able

able king of the Trinobantians; as, at the time of our meeting, there was nothing in my poffeffion worthy his acceptance. The fubjects reprefented in thefe paintings will furely receive his approbation: the one is Julius Cæfar, when very young, replacing the trophies of Marius, which had been thrown down by the reigning party of Sylla: the other, the fame hero in his tent, giving orders that the riches and effects of thofe who had deferted from his camp, fhould be fent after them. Amongft the officers who ftand near him, it was my defire that the figure of my grandfather fhould be faithfully taken from the excellent ftatue made of him during the Gallic war; and the painter has perfectly preferved his refemblance, as well as that of Cæfar. The pictures will foon be completed, and Lyfias had my fincere thanks for the mafterly and expreffive manner in which he has executed my ideas. He was much pleafed to find me fenfible of the

difficulty

difficulty he had furmounted, in adopting a fubject from the choice of another, and particularly of one who has no profeffional knowledge of the art. To this reafon he principally imputes that inequality obfervable in the works of men of genius; for it is not to be expected that any one can command the imagination of another, whofe talents muft be directed by his own judgment, or they will lofe a great portion of their efficacy. The mechanical part of this engaging ftudy is little when compared with the foul that fhould animate every figure, and which cannot be imparted if the ideas of the painter do not fully correfpond with the nature of the fubject.

Lyfias has no want of this animation; he feels with all the warmth of poetic fancy, and enters into every character he wifhes to delineate. He has now in hand feveral pictures defigned after Homer; and has

fucceeded

succeeded admirably in the firſt council and
diſpute between Agamemnon and Achilles.
Both theſe heroes exhibit the characteriſtic
touches, which diſtinguiſh them from each
other, and from the reſt of the Grecians ;
but this perfection has not been attained
without a nice examination into the whole
of their conduct, as deſcribed by the poet.
" It is not enough," ſays Lyſias, " that
a painter ſhould conſider with attention any
particular action which his colours are to
bring before the eyes ; he muſt be acquainted
with all the events relative to the perſons
who are to be actors in his piece, and with
the manner in which they were affected by
them : the ſame paſſions have more or leſs
effect upon different men, and influence them
in a very diverſified manner.   We muſt
know what have been their ſentiments and
their behaviour on other occaſions, before
we can decide what impreſſion any ſingle
circumſtance

circumstance could make on them. On the countenance of the dying Hipparchus *, it may be enough to reprefent terror and indignation; but in that of Cæfar, we muft denote the magnanimity of his character, by the fortitude with which he meets his fate, and by the look of generous contempt which he cafts on the confpirators; and if the painter can add to thefe the glance directed at Brutus, he may truly be efteemed a great, a fuperior artift!

" Few poets have afforded fuch ample matter for inftruction to a painter as Homer. Confidered in a moral fenfe, his Agamemnon and Achilles are faulty; but they are perfect, as characters juftly delineated from nature. Agamemnon, as painted by Homer, is an ambitious, vindictive prince; jealous of his authority, haughty to his officers, and kind

* Tyrant of Athens, killed by Harmodius and Ariftogiton.

to his troops; he is a tender brother, an excellent king, a man not readily tranfported by his paffions; but, from a high fenfe of honour, firm in his refentment, and yet induced by his defire of military fame, and by affection for his army, to make great fubmiffions to his private enemy; but fub-miffions which are not humiliating. He reftores Brifeis, whom he had only detained as a proof of his authority: he reftores her in fuch a manner as fhews his refpect for the laws of honour; but he openly declares, that Achilles has no right to fufpect him; and adds other prefents, by which he rather confers a favour, than acknowledges a fault."

" To the portrait given of Achilles by one of your poets," continued Lyfias, " it may be added that he was obedient to the duties and precepts of religion, generous in his refentment, divided by paffion and fenfibi-lity, attentive to the voice of reafon, and ftill more fo to the voice of honour; hurried too

far

far by every noble sentiment; but yielding
to the will of Calchas, from a consideration
of his being interpreter of the Gods; to the
will of his mother, from reverence and
filial affection; and, to the will of Patroclus,
from a high sense of the sacred ties of
friendship. Thus are his passions alternately actuated by his friends and his enemies,
while he appears, through the whole poem,
the victim of his excellent heart and violent
disposition.

" A want of delicacy and feeling in some
inferior artists has destroyed that nice dis-
crimination of character which forms the
great effect of the Iliad. Agamemnon must
not have the mien of a tyrant, nor Achilles
that of a madman; in Homer they are men
subject to error, but their characters are
respectable and interesting."

Lysias sets no bounds to his admiration of
Homer, and I think he describes with great

precision

precision the impression made on him by the principal figures of the Iliad.

He remarks that the astonishing diversity of characters in this poem can never be sufficiently admired; and that the nicety with which they are delineated, can only be compared to a picture executed with a perfect knowledge of perspective, where the gradations are distinctly marked and yet insensibly separated.

" What is very extraordinary," said he, " is the manner in which Agamemnon is distinguished from the rest; he is absolutely the sovereign, and no one who reads the Iliad can bear the supposition that any other chief could have been elected to command the army. His brother Menelaus is also distinctly drawn, so as to excite every interesting sentiment: the motives of his conduct seem entirely to spring from a sense of honour. No man of generosity would refuse to fight

for

for Menelaus; and though he has not the advantages of some of the other heroes, his behaviour always shews him deserving of, and grateful for their assistance. He appears in the field with sensibility and courage, and in the council with that placid dignity, and modest, though anxious attention, which agree with his situation and character."

The five characters of Ajax, Achilles, Diomedes, Ulysses, and Nestor, are most remarkably distinguished: the first is a perfect contrast to the last, and yet it is easy to perceive the chain that unites them. To continue the image of perspective; Ajax is like a figure on the fore-ground; his outline is strongly marked; force and strength are his characteristics; we admire in him all the skill of the artist, but he excites in us little interest for himself; and yet we dwell on him with pleasure, as his character does not wholly want attraction; and we might be

longer

longer detained, if the principal figure of Achilles did not command our attention. There we fee elegance, dignity, and vigour fet in the nobleft light: the beams that flafh from his helmet dazzle our eyes; his look penetrates the foul, and the expreffion of fenfibility in his countenance interefts us fo ftrongly, that it is long before we obferve the other figures. But when we defcend to thefe, with what fatisfaction we contemplate Diomedes; for, as in the heroic Achilles, the fierce and almoft brutal courage of Ajax appears to be purified from terreftrial drofs; and to receive the brighteft emanations of celeftial fire, fo in Diomedes the fury of Achilles is tempered into the calm and fteady intrepidity of the valiant foldier, and the experienced general. Diomedes is not a kind of celeftial being, like Achilles, but then he is the firft of mortals. Where is the man of warm imagination, who, at twenty, would not dream of being an Achilles, and

at

at thirty would not wish to be a Dio-
med?"

Lysias here paused for a reply; I assented
to his remarks, and he continued the same
image.

" After these," said he, " the figures retreat
to the back-ground, but they are still infinitely
beautiful. Ulysses is painted with the greatest care; the shining valour of Achilles, the
steady courage of the son of Tydeus, obscure
indeed the military talents of Ulysses; but
his figure is pleasing, the proportions are just
and learnedly marked: without him there
would be a dreadful void, and we perceive
that for this portrait greater skill has been
required, as for the others more imagination.
Beyond him is Nestor, mellowed into the
soft gravity of age, yet rising like a majestic
and awful pyramid, to terminate the scene
of dignity. Here we must again observe the
wonderful discernment, or, perhaps, sensibi-

lity of Homer; one step beyond Nestor a figure would have degenerated into the weakest dotage; one line beyond Ajax it would have swelled into deformity and madness."

You must, I hope, be satisfied, my friend, with the relation here given of my conversation with Lysias, from which you may see that I do not voluntarily exclude from my mind what may suspend its disquietude. Suffer me now to inform you of a circumstance which at once renewed my anxiety. After viewing the unfinished paintings, I desired to see those which were completed; and Lysias led me into another room, where I observed, in the figure of Andromache parting from Hector, a striking likeness of Valeria. Upon my enquiry whether it was intended for a portrait, Lysias answered, it was not: but said, that whenever he met any person, whose elegance of features, or dignity

of

of form, coincided with the ideas in his mind of the heroes or heroines defcribed by the poets, his memory faithfully affifted him to exprefs the image at his return to his ftudies.   I defired to be the purchafer of this picture, but he informed me that it was promifed to Drufus.

I need not tell you, Septimius, how great was my mortification; I left the painter immediately, and went to enquire whether Drufus was returned. I fcarce knew what I fhould have faid to him; but certainly I fhould have complained to him for interfering in the concerns of a family, who would rather glorioufly perifh with the commonwealth, than be reftored to their ancient rights through the felfifh interpofition of the fon of their ruler. I have yet obtained no intelligence of Drufus: and furely his abfence, at this time, can admit of no favourable conftruction. It was his duty, as a

    man

man of honour, to take the earlieſt opportunity of explaining to me the motives from
which he had acted in ſo extraordinary a
manner.

LET.

I HAVE reafon to hope, my friend, that the legates of Maroboduus will be difmiffed without fucceeding in the purpofe of their embaffy ; but they have not yet received their final anfwer. Our ftate will undoubtedly fhew that we have ftill public virtue fufficient to defpife the little arts of fomenting, or of even deriving advantage from the internal difcord of our enemies. Whatever corruption may be diffeminated through Rome, by the prefent fyftem of government, and by the increafe of wealth and luxury, we are ftill noble in our conduct to foreign nations, and generous to thofe who have a juft claim to our affiftance.

You will have heard of the tremendous

M 3

earth-

earthquake, which has overthrown twelve flourishing cities of Afia. One night of horror has deftroyed the lives and properties of innumerable citizens: the face of nature has been changed; mountains have been tranfported far from their priftine fituation; and wide extended plains have difappeared from the face of day. A dreadful conflagration has confumed what the fhock of warring elements, and the convulfion of the earth, had fpared; and thofe who have efcaped the general defolation, are reduced to the extremeft want and mifery. Tiberius and the fenate have unanimoufly decreed to fuccour thefe unfortunate people with large fums of money, and neceffaries for their prefent fubfiftence; to grant them a remiffion of taxes for the fpace of five years, and every indulgence that can alleviate their diftreffes. The emperor has diftinguifhed himfelf in liberality towards them, and a fenator, of prætorian rank, is deputed to vifit the fcene

of

of thefe calamities. Univerfal Rome applauds the decrees; and Tiberius has made
a greater progrefs in the affection of the Romans, by his care of thefe diftant fufferers,
than if he had beftowed millions in the city.
Generous nation! may you never lofe this
liberality of fentiment! The wreaths of con-
queft are indeed an ornament to the brows
that fhine with univerfal benevolence! While
humanity directs our councils, victory will
attend our arms! Septimius, you will exult
with me more than ever at being born a
Roman!

This is not the only proof which Tiberius
has lately given of his juftice and propriety
of conduct: he watches ftrictly over the execution of his fumptuary laws: he refufes all
inheritances, except thofe which he has deferved by friendfhip, and has beftowed on indigent nobles the fortunes which, for want
of heirs, would have fallen to the prince. He
has difmiffed, or fuffered to depart, from the

fenate

senate those who, by their libertinism and dissipation, have profusely squandered their revenues, and stooped to mean and unworthy resources. O my friend! why is not a great prince always a man of virtue? If the private character of Tiberius was equal to his talents for government, we should less regret the loss of liberty.

Germanicus informed him of all we knew relative to Philocles, and the emperor listened with attention to his narrative; but though it is scarcely possible that he should confide in him after such information, yet I fear I am not deceived by those who declare that the Greek has frequent audiences of Tiberius. The fatal dissimulation of the sovereign, which creates his own misery, and raises perpetual mistrust in those who would willingly nourish an affection for him, poisons even the good that might flow from his counsels, or attend his actions. He keeps me in the most painful suspense

till

till Valerius arrives; nevertheless, I must acknowledge that there is no probability of his dissembling in this particular, and that my alarms are rather for the future, than the present. All the senators, and most of the principal citizens of Rome, have made me visits of congratulation; and, what is singular, Sejanus has been of the number: but him I did not receive.

My uncle would not be recalled in so public a manner, if the emperor had any present design inimical to his safety: my opinion is, that he wishes to bring him over to his party, or at least to prevent his supporting those who oppose the designs of power. Many hints, that have been dropped in conversation, by some of the patricians most in favour, convince me that my suspicions are not groundless; but as I know how firmly Valerius will adhere to his ancient principles, I am not without disquietude on the effect which such a disappoint-

ment.

ment in his hopes may have on the difpofition of Tiberius. His notions of honour
and equity have ever been fo pliant to his
interefts, that he can have little faith in the
integrity of other men. I am perfuaded
that if the emperor was perfectly affured of
the fincerity and probity of Valerius; if
he credited what I folemnly declared when
I firft addreffed him, after my return from
Ericufa, and what the whole tenor of my
uncle's conduct might have demonftrated,
that he is only the friend of Rome, and
not the enemy of Tiberius; if he was certain of this invariable truth, he would not
feek the ruin of a man whofe talents and
reputation are the firmeft fupport of juft
and lawful authority. Perhaps he is at
length convinced: I wifh to fuppofe him
capable of a belief in virtue, not only for
the fafety of Valerius, but for the profperity of my country.

LETTER

I AM juſt now returned from Tibur*; Sigiſmar was deſirous to ſee me, and I could not refuſe his requeſt, though every hour of my abſence from Rome has increaſed my impatience in the fear of delaying the ſatisfaction I ſhould experience in receiving accounts of Valerius. The time approaches in which I may hope for his return, and this was ſo ſtrong a motive to detain me at Rome, that I had almoſt reſolved not to yield, till after his arrival, to the earneſt entreaties of Sigiſmar, to be at leaſt for a few hours a witneſs of his felicity. But as I had received early this morning intelligence from Oſtia,

* Tivoli, a ſmall city and biſhoprick near Rome.

that

that no veſſel was in fight, and that not a breath of wind was ſtirring, I determined to paſs the day with my friend, and was received by him with unſpeakable kindneſs. Bertha ſeemed no leſs delighted with my viſit, and treated me with that frank and unreſerved affection, which can only flow from a heart conſcious of its own purity and innocence. She was not embarraſſed by my preſence, nor any further elated than was natural at the fight of a friend who is equally dear to herſelf and her huſband; a huſband, during whoſe abſence many intereſting and important events have happened to us all. She preſented to me her lovely infant, with a ſmile of pleaſure and ſerenity, and ſpoke of Sigiſmar with ſuch tenderneſs and eſteem, as convinced me that ſhe is worthy of partaking with him a life of virtuous happineſs: they are enchanted with their new habitation, and the country round them. If Sigiſmar could be aſſured that peace would

ſubſiſt

fubfift between the Romans and his countrymen, I am apt to believe that he would
defire no other refidence.

You remember the fituation of the villa on
the moft elevated part of the hill near the
entrance of the town, expofed to the fetting
fun, and fhaded to the eaft by a wood of
olives. I do not recollect that you ever
entered the gardens, which are extenfive, and
ornamented with a greater number of fhrubs
and flowers than ftatues or vafes. There is,
however, in a grove of myrtle, a young
fawn, playing on a double flute, which is
allowed to have confiderable merit. From
the terrace are different views of the city of
Tibur, of the cafcades, Mount Catillus, and
the ferpentine courfe of the Anio*. The
arable land and the vineyards are in good
order, and equal to any poffeffions in the
neighbourhood. There is a fmall library in

---

* Now called the Tiverone.

the houfe, confifting chiefly of poetical or hiftorical works. I found Sigifmar reading to Bertha the elegies of Tibullus; Vercennis was gone to the temple of the Sybil*; after fhe returned, and we had fpent fome time in mutual demonftrations of regard, many tears were fhed to the memory of Cariovaldas, whofe image was prefent to me, whenever I looked on the united family, to whofe happinefs was only wanting this great and good man, who had facrificed his life to fave that of Sigifmar and Flaminius. Septimius! you will conceive how much I regretted that it was denied me to return him, in this place, that hofpitality which I fo long experienced under his roof. To-morrow I will give orders for the erection of a monument, which fhall perpetuate my gratitude and his virtues. In the afternoon I walked down into the valley with Sigifmar; and felt

* See Horace, Od. vii. lib. 1.

anew all the pleafing fenfations, which I ufed to experience when wandering along the banks of the refounding Anio before my departure for Germany.   The variety of trees, the magnificent edifices that raife their lofty heads amidft the rural beauties of the fcene, the murmur of the cafcades, the fragrance diffufed by an inexhauftible variety of flowers and aromatic plants, the coolnefs communicated by the zephyrs from the light vapour that rifes out of the falling waters and extends over all the valley; the awful dignity of the mountains, that defend it from the noxious winds, and leave to the weft an exten-five view of the Roman plains; every thing contributes to the pleafures of this moft delightful retreat of our poets, and the favourite fcene of their contemplations. I revifited the fumptuous villa where Mecænas* was fur-

* The friend of Auguftus; the ruins of his villa are eminently picturefque.

rounded by the happieft votaries of the Mufes; where Auguftus received, in friendfhip, an alleviation of the cares of empire; and in immortal verfe, the reward of his actions, with the confecration of his fame to remoteft pofterity; and yet Mecænas was not the friend, for whom, were I a fovereign, I fhould moft envy Auguftus. Agrippa is he whofe character does the greateft honour to that prince, and to himfelf. How little might we expect to fee a man preferve the confidence of a friend, who had been raifed by him to the higheft fummit of human greatnefs, when that friend ftood no longer in need of his affiftance? And how little might we expect that man to be content with the honours beftowed on him, and think his fervices fufficiently rewarded? Yet, fuch was Agrippa; who never gave advice that did not tend to the good of his country, nor fought any other recompenfe than the confcioufnefs of his own virtues. Mecænas was a lefs active, and lefs deter-

mined

mined character; but his mildnefs and clemency of difpofition, the humanity he difplayed in his influence over Auguftus, the diftinguifhed protection which he granted to men of learning, or rather the familiar intercourfe in which he lived with them, the tafte and difcernment with which he felected the moft deferving, and the conftancy of his attachments, are qualities that muft for ever render his name dear and valuable. None will repine at the fplendor of a villa, no lefs the feat of inftruction and benevolence, than of elegance and pomp.

We afterwards walked round to the other fide of the valley: I fhewed my friend the fimple dwelling* where Horace put in practice thofe maxims of content, and neglect, of riches which he inculcates in fuch harmonious numbers, and with a fincerity unufual not only to the poet, but to the philo-

---

* Horace's villa at Tivoli is generally fuppofed to have been fituated near the church of St. Anthony.

fopher. With the fame truth he fung that he could not furvive Mecænas, and the event proved that he felt the friendfhip he defcribed.

I was greatly affected at the fight of the villa of Quintilius Varus *. Valerius had introduced me to him here a fhort time before I accompanied him on his laft fatal expedition; I felt anew the horrors of his fate, and could not, without difcompofure, anfwer the queftions of Sigifmar, who enquired after the proprietor of this magnificent habitation. I haftily walked forward, and quitted the place with a figh.

We were now arrived at the oaks of Tiburnus, and the manfion where dwelt the beauteous Cynthia, whom Propertius has taken fo much pains to celebrate, or defame. We returned at fun-fet to join Vercennis and Bertha, who had decorated the hall,

* Confiderable ruins of his villa ftill remain, and the chapel near it is called by the peafants la Madonna di Quintiliolo.

where

where we were to take our repaft, with garlands and vafes of the frefheft flowers. At length I bade farewell to this tranquil fcene of domeftic enjoyment, and returned to Rome immerfed in lonely and penfive melancholy.

———

This inftant has made me the happieft of mortals; I have received a letter written by Valerius, dated from Caïeta, which leaves me no doubt of the certainty of his return. Though he does not appear confcious that I can entertain any fufpicions, it is plain that his paternal goodnefs has difpatched this exprefs to calm my mind: he was to weigh anchor the fame night, and may foon arrive at Oftia; to-morrow I fhall go thither; every moment of happinefs is precious: I fhould not pardon myfelf were I to mifs the firft appearance of the fails that waft hither Valerius, and his enchanting daughter.

I WRITE to you from Oftia, my friend, but there is yet no appearance of the gallies of Valerius.   Before I left Rome this morning, I went to the fculptor Polidore, to give directions for the monument of Cariovaldas. You know my partiality for ftatuary, and need not now be told of my unlimited veneration and gratitude for the memory of that excellent man.   I fhould therefore fet no bounds to the magnificence of the cenotaph, were I merely to confult my own inclination ;. but pompous tombs are ufually confidered rather as proofs of the vanity of thofe who erect them, than of refpect for the dead, or memorials of their virtues.   As I have no portrait of Cariovaldas, I cannot perpetuate his features,

and

and muft therefore content myfelf with expreffing, as far as poffible, the fentiments
and genius with which they were animated.
It is agreed that this monument fhall confift
of a lofty column of porphyry of the Doric
order; the bafe to be of the pureft Parian
marble, and the focle of bafalt.   The weftern
front of the pedeftal is to bear an infcription,
delineating the character of Cariovaldas,
and relating the circumftances of his death.
To the eaft will. be a bafs-relief of confiderable fize, reprefenting Fortitude guided by
Minerva, who embraces with one hand the
ftatue of Germany, placed on the altar of
patriotifm, and contemplates, with benevolent fmiles, a globe of the world, prefented to
her by Humanity.   On the right fide of the
pedeftal is to be a trophy of the various arms
in ufe among the Germans, intwined with
wreaths of laurel; and on the left are to be
placed two figures, reprefenting Sigifmar and
myfelf fixing a civic crown on a funereal urn.
This cenotaph I mean to erect on the moft

N 3   elevated

elevated ſpot of the gardens, now inhabited by the family of Cariovaldas; a place which I earneſtly deſire to appropriate to them and theirs for ever.

You are too well acquainted with the maſterly performances of Polidore, to doubt of the perfection with which this idea will be executed. My pleaſure and admiration are inexpreſſibly excited by the grace and ſimplicity that diſtinguiſh his works, and the ſoul with which they appear to be animated. I was this morning particularly charmed with an Apollo *, whoſe attitude and countenance repreſent that majeſtic ſcorn with which Ovid makes him addreſs the God of Love, immediately after the deſtruction of the ſerpent Python. The figure is ſingularly beautiful, and the ſame poetic fire which dictated the lines, you may ſo well remember, ſeems to have infuſed itſelf into the ſculptor. A group of Laocöon †, with his two ſons,

* † The ideas of the reader will naturally recur to the Laocöon and Apollo of the Belvidere, but it is generally

thought

in vain endeavouring to defend themſelves from the ſerpents that are twined around them, next caught my attention ; the execution of this dreadful ſubject is wonderful; but arts, which are intended to adorn and ſoften life, ſhould not, ſurely, be applied to images of horror. The ſkill of the artiſt is indeed more viſible in diſtorted features, and limbs writhing in the agony of pain ; but, perhaps, greater genius is required to give a juſt and natural expreſſion of the gentle paſſions of the ſoul. Sentiments are more difficult to repreſent than actions ; and I am perſuaded the Apollo required deeper ſtudy than

thought they were of a later date in Rome. Pliny writes that the Laocöon was the work of three celebrated Rhodians, Ageſander, Polidore, and Athenedorus, and that it was placed in the palace of Titus : the Belvedere Apollo was found at Nettuno. Mr. Addiſon, in his travels, remarks, that the moſt ancient medal, on which it is repreſented, is one of Antoninus Pius. It is well-known that the ſame ſubject was often repeated with little variation by ancient ſculptors, and the author does not pretend to fix the date of any ſtatue now exiſting.

N 4 the

the Laocöon, though, at firſt ſight, the ſpec-
tator forms a very different judgment.
Polidore aſſures me that various ſculptors
have already made excellent copies of the
latter, but none have yet ſucceeded in imitating the Apollo.

I was infinitely pleaſed with his remark
on the different taſte he had obſerved in the
Romans and the Greeks. " Before I left
my native country," ſaid he, " I was chiefly
employed on ſubjects merely fabulous or
ideal: the metamorphoſis of various Deities,
the repreſentation of Tritons and Syrens,
Sphinxes, and Chimæras, ſeduce the lively
imagination of the Grecian, but rarely ſatisfy
the mind or judgment of a Roman. With you
the portrait of a friend, the repreſentation of
any hiſtorical fact, in which courage or generoſity is diſplayed, the image of a hero or
a ſage, are the objects of univerſal approbation.
Rome triumphant, allegorical figures, that
denote ſome favourite virtue, or the attributes

of

of a conquered province, are all the efforts of fancy that pleafe your countrymen. Amongft the Gods, Jupiter, Mars, and Cupid are thofe you moft frequently defire; but the Greeks delight in novelty, and recommended by this, the moft capricious compofition engages their attention. The Romans are not eafily wearied with a repetition of the fame fubject, if it has once interefted them; but whatever exceeds propriety, or probability, excites their difguft. I have formed my tafte in Greece, and corrected it in Italy."

I know not, Septimius, but it may be in confequence of this difpofition that we generally prefer fculpture to painting. The illufion of colouring is far more fenfible than that of form, and there requires much lefs exertion of the fancy to be fatisfied with a ftatue than with a picture. The former has ufually more the appearance of nature and fimplicity; art is more manifeft in the

latter.

latter. The Roman temples abound in figures of bronze and marble, which imprefs us with more fublime ideas of dignity, than the variety of colours requifite in painting, however harmonioufly combined. Perhaps the notion of folidity may contribute fome-thing to the preference: we always wifh our actions to be immortal, and this wifh has often made them worthy of eternal fame. The Grecian lives more for himfelf and his contemporaries; the Roman, for his coun-try and for pofterity.

Great have been the virtues of the Greeks; but the ficklenefs of their difpofition, the inftability of their councils, and, in every refpect, their immoderate love of change, render ufelefs to their country the extraordi-nary talents, and indefatigable induftry, with which nature and education have endowed them. The Spartans alone, unfhaken in their principles, and conftant to their inftitutions,

tutions, long refifted the pernicious influence of example, and the reiterated affaults
of jealous enmity. The Spartans muft be
revered as long as heroifm is honoured, or
virtue beloved.

SEPTIMIUS, you have long been the part-
ner of my afflictions; I now entreat you to
participate of the pureft, the fublimeft joy—
Valerius is reftored to his country!

Soon after I had finished my laft letter, the
gallies, which conducted him, appeared
in fight. I inftantly went out to meet them,
and found him neither elated nor difcom-
pofed by his change of fortune. He received me with his ufual tendernefs; but
gently rebuked me for the immoderate tranfport which I had no power to fupprefs. Valeria was greatly affected, and the fenators
who accompanied them, were far from being
indifferent fpectators of our meeting. When
the gallies entered the port, innumerable

crowds

crowds of people covered the fhore, and the multitude increafed as we approached nearer to Rome.   Every demonftration of zeal and affection that a nation can beftow, was accumulated on Valerius ; and his entrance into the city had more the refemblance of a triumph, than of a return from exile.   All his relations, and many of the other principal nobility of Rome, were at his houfe to wait his arrival, having received information that the gallies were in fight of Oftia. During the whole of that day and the following morning, the manfion was thronged with vifitants, and re-echoed with congratulations.   This was but a prelude to what followed : how can I defcribe to you, my friend, his firft appearance in the fenate ? Thanks to Auguftus * who reftored to young patricians the privilege of attending the debates of this auguft affembly ! I was prefent at his entrance, and would not have loft the

* Life of that Emperor.

advantage

advantage of being a spectator, at this triumphant moment, for the empire of the universe. Every senator arose and welcomed Valerius; every countenance displayed the various passions with which the mind was agitated. The felicitations of the good and sincere were warm, but delivered in few words; their looks expressed more than their tongues; while the flatterers of Tiberius, and the adherents of Sejanus, distinguished themselves by long and exaggerated praises. Valerius answered the first with affection, and the latter with dignity. The universal sentiments appeared to be those of respect and veneration: he took his place, and the numerous assembly were hushed to general silence: all eyes were fixed on him, and every other thought seemed suspended in attention to what he was about to utter. He arose with that grace and majesty, which are natural to him, and began by thanking the senate for the welcome with which one of its members had been

received

received, after a long and extraordinary absence. He said, that his constant and uni-
form adherence to the duties imposed on
every individual who was called to so distinguished a part in the government of his
country, gave him reason to hope that no
one present would suspect him of having
voluntarily relinquished the station in which
the will of the immortal Gods, and his zeal
for the welfare of Rome, had placed him.
He then related, with dispassionate concise-
ness, the circumstances attending his con-
veyance to the island of Ericusa, the manner
of his living there, and the means by which
I had discovered the place of his retreat. He
barely mentioned, without animadversion,
the accusations with which the slaves had
loaded Sejanus; and having concluded his
narrative, he proceeded thus:

" I am not conscious of having merited,
either by my private or public conduct, the
resentment of the injured, or the attacks of

the

the malignant; the whole tenor of my life has been invariably directed to the service of my country; I have vindicated her honour in the field, and her laws and liberties in this affembly. I have oppofed none but the favourers of fedition and fervility; I look on no man as my enemy, but the enemies of Rome; and will acknowledge none for my friend, who is not animated by the fame fentiment.

" I hope it will not be interpreted as a want of gratitude towards you, confcript fathers! who were pleafed to depute two of the moft refpectable and moft illuftrious characters in Rome to recal me to this temple; nor towards the auguft prince who convoked you for this purpofe, and who firft propofed my return, if I declare, that divefting myfelf of my public character, my exile was neither injurious nor painful. Happy in the fociety of a daughter, who to the purity of a veftal unites the fortitude of

a heroine;

a heroine; accompanied by satisfactory re-flections on my past conduct, on the esteem of this venerable assembly, and on .the af-fection of my fellow citizens, for my zeal in the support of their interests, and of the principles in the Valerian family; the event that separated me from those honours granted by the Roman people, was not capable of interrupting that serenity, which nothing but a consciousness of guilt could ever have banished from my breast.

" But though Titus Valerius has neither been injured nor offended; conscript fathers! a senator of Rome has been illegally trans-ported by his slaves to a remote and miserable island.   He has been debarred the enjoy-ment of those rights to which every member of this assembly is entitled.   Your dignity has been insulted, and this example proves that rank does not secure you from the insidious or daring attempts of your enemies or dependants.   I will not condemn a citizen

of Rome on the teſtimony of three guilty
ſlaves, who can exhibit no proofs of ſe-
duction; neither will I demand the puniſh-
ment of theſe ſlaves, becauſe it is impoſſible
to judge how far they may have been intimidated or corrupted. I therefore propoſe,
and earneſtly requeſt of every ſenator who
loves his country to join his ſuffrage to mine,
that an act of oblivion may take place for all
the proceedings which have been either attempted or effected againſt Titus Valerius."

He was here interrupted by an univerſal
murmur, and many voices were diſtinguiſhed
that exclaimed, "No man who loves his
country can ſuffer that iniquity to remain
unpuniſhed, which has conſpired againſt
her nobleſt ornament."

Valerius entreated ſilence and then reſumed
his ſpeech:

"Conſcript fathers! permit me to proceed, and if ever I merited your approbation
attend to my requeſt. To this act of oblivion,

vion, I propofe fhall be added a decree for the obfervance of the ancient laws, by which no fenator is allowed to abfent himfelf from his duty without giving a full and diftinct account of the motives which oblige him to retire; and that if any future attempt of the fame nature, as that which now excites your indignation, fhould be difcovered, the agents, authors, and abettors of the fame fhall be punifhed as traitors to their coun- try."

The acclamations were now fo loud that it was long before the fubject could be difcuffed with any degree of calmnefs; at length after a long debate, in which it was remarkable that the known enemies of liberty were thofe who moft vehemently demanded the punifhment of the offenders, a confiderable majority decided for the opi- nion of Valerius.

He expreffed his thanks in the warmeft manner for the deference paid to his pro-

pofal,

pofal, and added that he fhould preferve no other remembrance of his exile, than what might tend to excite his fenfibility for the marks of affection with which his country had honoured his return. "I have now," faid he, "acknowledged, though imperfectly, my obligations to Cæfar, to this venerable fenate, and to the citizens of Rome in general: I muft next acquit myfelf of my private obligations. Marcus Quintius Flaminius, on whofe merits and fervices I will forbear to enlarge; not in fear of being fufpected of partiality towards the fon of a beloved fifter, but becaufe they are recently and publicly known, is the perfon to whom I particularly owe my reftoration to this affembly, and to the fervice of my country. Attached to his duty, and to the glory of the Roman arms, he fuppreffed his filial folicitude till repeated victories authorized his return to Italy: he then with indefatigable piety, and unremitting affiduity fought, and,

at

at length, difcovered the place of my retreat. I recommend him, confcript fathers! to your notice: he has fhewn himfelf worthy of your protection and of the name he bears; in you may he find a powerful and parental fupport, when Valerius is no more; and may he juftify this application, by proving himfelf no lefs the defender of your rights, than the glorious avenger of the infulted dignity of Rome, and the fortunate reftorer of her facred enfigns!"

Septimius, I fhould vainly endeavour to relate what I now felt, or what paffed in the fenate. Let it fuffice that you are informed nothing could exceed the demonftrations of regard with which your friend was honoured by the fathers of his country. It will ever be confidered by me as the moft awful period in my paft life, and the goodnefs of Valerius had almoft deprived me of the power of utterance."

He continued: " Confcript fathers! you

O 3 know

know my heart, and can judge how deeply it
is affected with a fenfe of your benefits.
Allow me to trefpafs a little longer on your
patience.   The Cherufcan warrior, with
whom Marcus Flaminius is connected by
reciprocal obligations, actuated by gratitude
and friendfhip, left his native country to inform him of the place of my exile, which he
difcovered by the means you have heard me
relate: his father, one of the chiefs of
that nation, treated with hofpitality your
fellow citizen, and at length preferved
his life by the facrifice of his own.   I therefore entreat that his fon may enjoy an honour
of which he is deferving: I would wifh that
he might obtain the freedom of this city,
and be raifed to the dignity of a Roman
knight.   No man is a greater afferter of the
majefty of our ftate, nor more cautious than
myfelf of communicating fo exalted a diftinction: I would fooner counfel the diftribution of treafures and provinces, than to
proftitute the honour of the Roman people,

by

by admitting unworthy sharers of their sacred privileges; but the virtues of this Cheruscan are congenial to our principles, and the man of courage and probity deserves to be a Roman. I therefore shall desire that the freedom of this city may be granted to Sigismar, son of the late Cariovaldas, with permission to assume the name of Titus Valerius. I should be concerned to omit informing you, conscript fathers! of any whose good offices have co-operated in the restoration of one of your colleagues, and if any such omission may have happened, I request that you will put a favourable construction on my sentiments."

I perceived that Germanicus, who was present at this meeting of the senate, seemed particularly attentive to these concluding words of Valerius, which manifestly regarded the interference of Drusus.

The business of the day being completed, my uncle, attended by a very considerable

O 4

number

number of fenators, went to the palace, and
was received by Tiberius with great apparent
regard. Sigifmar, with his family, is to be
enrolled amongft the citizens of Rome ; and
this privilege delivers Bertha from the power
of Ingomar. The other hoftages are to be
fent back with the ambaffadors, who will
not obtain any affiftance againft Arminius.
Immediately after having accompanied Valerius in his vifit to the emperor, I returned
home, to give you a narration of the proceedings of the day, and to acquaint Sigifmar
with the certain profpect of peace between
his country and ours, previous to the information of his becoming our fellow citizen.

As the games of the Circus * begin to-
morrow, Valerius intends to avail himfelf of
this opportunity to pafs a few days at his
villa near Prænefte †. He wifhes to avoid

* Roman calendar.

† Paleftrina, a fmall city and bifhoprick in the Pope's
ftates, a fief of the Barberini family.

the

the concourfe of vifitants that continually
fill his apartments, and to allot fome time
for domeftic and focial enjoyments.   Marcus
Lepidus *, his approved and excellent friend,
is to accompany him, and he has granted me
the fame permiffion.   I have an important
fuit to obtain from his paternal goodnefs;
he is not ignorant of my attachment to Valeria, and I dare flatter myfelf that he will
foon confent to fecure my happinefs.

* Tacitus, Book 1. and 4.

LET-

THE British princes, grandsons of the venerable Mandubratius, are arrived; and Germanicus, to whom their visit is principally intended, has desired that I would assist him in shewing them every attention of friendship and hospitality. This circumstance, which would have given me infinite satisfaction at any other time, is now a source of mortification, as it has prevented me from accompanying Valerius to Prænefte.

They are charged by the king of the Trinobantians, to congratulate Tiberius, and the Roman people, on the success of our arms between the Rhine and Albis, and to offer gifts in the temple of Jupiter Capitolinus. Before my return from

Ericufa,

Ericufa, Cornelius Dolabella was fent to meet them at the port of Luna *, where they firft difembarked on their arrival from Gaul. It was their choice to continue the voyage by fea, and they came up the Tiber, attended by a great number of veffels richly ornamented, amidft the acclamations of the Roman people, who are interefted in their favour on account of the generous conduct of their parent and fovereign towards thofe of our fellow-foldiers who fuffered fhip-wreck on his coaft.

As foon as I heard of their arrival, I left the field of Mars, where I was exercifing, and having entered a barge with fome other friends of Germanicus, we joined them at a little diftance from the city. They were tranfported to fee me, and were eager in their enquiries concerning the objects prefented to their view, as we advanced up the river.

* Gulph della Spezia.

They

They particularly admired the Naumachia *, and gardens of Cæsar, with the numberless villas that adorn the Janicule hill; the next instant they turned their eyes to the Aventine, and I had scarcely time to answer the variety of their questions, being obliged to tell them the name and destination of every building which they saw. The temples † of Diana and Juno, the grove of laurels, with the sepulchre of Tatius, the fane of liberty, and the public library of Asinius Pollio, the cave of the robber Cacus, and the history of Evander, were all to be explained. But what singularly engaged their attention was the Sublician bridge ‡, which has acquired such celebrity from the heroic act of Hora-

* Now St. Cosimato and villa Barcrini.

† These temples, &c. are mentioned by many ancient authors: the priory of Malta, St. Alexis, and Santa Sabina, are built on their ruins.

‡ The remains of this still to be seen under the priory of Malta.

tius

tius Cocles. When we arrived at the ifland *, I was unwilling to enter into any details, for you may imagine that I had no inclination to recount the progrefs of the God of Phyfic from Epidaurus in the form of a ferpent, or the confecration of the place where he thought proper to fix his abode. I fhould be much more difpofed to look on this ifland as facred on account of its formation. It is undoubtedly a remarkable monument of that integrity which would not fuffer our forefathers to appropriate to their own ufe the treafures of a tyrant whom they had exiled, nor the product of an eftate which they had confecrated to Mars. But this was not a narration for the ear of princes: the name of Tarquin is an infult to monarchs, and fhould not be pronounced in the prefence

* Now called Ifland of St. Bartholomew, from the church of that name; there is ftill an hofpital called De buon Fratelli.

of

of, thofe whofe dominion is founded on equity, and on the love of their people. I therefore contented myfelf with pointing out to the Britifh youths the temple of Efculapius, with the adjoining hofpital, not omitting to mention the ftatue of Julius Cæfar, whofe memory is fo interefting to them.

Germanicus employs, for the entertainment of his guefts, every opportunity afforded by his ftation, with all the urbanity and amiable beneficence of his difpofition. It is not in the nature of the emperor to receive any one with kindnefs, but he confers on thefe every honour which ftate and magnificence can beftow. They are to be introduced into the fenate, with peculiar diftinction, as foon as the games are finifhed; and in the mean while they are highly delighted with the races and other amufements incidental to the feafon.

This

This morning they were prefent at the dedication of the temple of Janus[*], erected by Caius Duilius, after his victory over the Carthaginians, the firft naval conqueror who graces the Roman annals. The edifice had fuffered fo much from the injuries of time, that Auguftus thought proper to rebuild it; and Tiberius has had the honour of newly confecrating it to the Deity whofe name it bears. The princes do not attend any of our rites without enquiring into their origin; and were greatly interefted by the hiftory of Duilius, and of our firft naval preparations againft the enemy, at that time mafter of the feas.

"We are iflanders," exclaimed they, with all the ardor of patriotifm; " the ocean muft be for us the field of action. Nature has given us ports and bays that feem to indicate our deftination; the winds that

* Tacitus, Book 2.

guard our coafts, impel our fails to con-
queft and dominion. We have the lofty and
venerable oak, which our Druids teach us to
behold with reverential awe; but thefe facred
trees may, indeed, become the guardians of
our ifle, when we convert them into floating
citadels and defenfive bulwarks. The naval
crown awaits us; and many a Briton may
hereafter emulate, if not furpafs, the glory
of Duilius."

Thefe youths are indued with a noble
pride, that endears them to every Roman;
and this difpofition, among many inftances,
appeared in the following fpeech made by
the youngeft to a fenator, who gave them
yeflerday a fumptuous banquet, at which
various ftrangers were prefent. " I obferve," faid he, " that the inhabitants of
different regions are received at Rome with
kindnefs and fplendor: you are fuperior to
the illiberal prejudices arifing from envy or
diftruft: you grant your protection to the
univerfe;

univerfe; but is there no nation worthy of your friendfhip? If you knew the hearts of the Britons, you would find them congenial with your own, and would beftow on them this honourable diftinction."

Thefe words were highly applauded, and had the defired effect on the hearers. There was not a Roman in company but bore tefti-, mony that he felt for thefe brave iflanders the fentiments which they wifhed to infpire.

Farewell, my dear Septimius, I have yet no account of Drufus. It is furely very ftrange that he has not returned to Rome for the celebration of the games *, he who is fo paffionately addicted to thefe amufements. What can be the motive of his abfence?

* Dion Caffius, Tacitus, &c.

I HAVE had the happiness, my friend, of passing some hours with Valerius and his amiable daughter. The British princes willingly accepted my proposal of accompanying them to Præneste. They had heard of the celebrated temple of Fortune *, consecrated by Sylla to the Goddess, whom he esteemed his protectress; and I conducted them to the villa of my uncle, which is delightfully situated near that of the emperor†, at a small distance from the city, and en-

---

* Plutarch, &c.

† Magnificent remains of the emperor's villa are still to be seen near Palestrine: the inhabitants calls it Villa Adriana, because the emperor Adrian enlarged it considerably: there is now a hermitage with a small chapel in the midst of the ruins.

joys

joys every advantage of this pure and salu-
brious air.

Valerius received them with his accuftomed
hofpitality and opennefs of manners.   As
he interefts himfelf warmly in promoting the
great object of their travels, which is to enlighten and improve their native country by
the knowledge they may acquire, he encouraged them in this noble defign, and at the
fame time gave them every caution againft
the feductions, which luxury has introduced
amongft us.

" Let not the delights of Hefperia," faid
he to thefe ingenuous youths, " induce you
to neglect the more folid advantages which
you may reap from a change of fcene. This
temporary abfence from the kingdom which,
by your birth, you are allotted to grace with
your refidence and adorn with your virtues,
may be effentially beneficial to yourfelves
and to your countrymen, if you make good
ufe of the time deftined for fuch purpofe ; but

if, dazzled by the fplendor of our capital,
or led aftray by its allurements, you fet too
high a value on enjoyments of which a few
revolving months would prove the fallacy,
you will return to Britain without any increafe of knowledge, and with a confidence
unworthy of your genuine character. You
will repine at the lofs of pleafures, the novelty of which was their greateft charm; you
will be diffatisfied with the virtuous fimplicity of your former life,-and perhaps fow
the fatal feeds óf corruption and mifery.
Forgive me, princes, for the fuppofition;
your native virtues, and the precepts of the
excellent Mandubratius muft furely fecure
you from the delufion incidental to other travellers ; you will tranfplant into your ifland
the laudable inftitutions of our forefathers;
the learning that makes men wife and good;
the exact difcipline, the manly eloquence,
and lofty fentiments that form the real
greatnefs of this nation : in courage and
                                        gene-

generosity you have already proved your-
selves our equals."

The youths seem desirous to follow the
instructions of Valerius: they examine with
attention every object worthy of their curiosity, and make diligent enquiries into
our laws, our government, and the annals
of our republic. No sooner did the sultry
heat of the day begin to abate, than they
grew impatient to visit the ancient city of
Præneste, and though I would gladly have
prolonged the happiness I felt in the conversation of Valeria, I was obliged to comply
with their desires.

As we approached near the hill, my
uncle, who accompanied us, gave the
princes a short account of the foundation of
Præneste, and the early part of its history.

" The* various edifices dependent on the

* In the prince's palace is to be seen a curious painting
by Pietro di Cortona, representing the ancient temple,
as he had collected the form of it from the ruins. The
altar for drawing the lots, &c. is now in the seminary.

                fane,"

fane," added he, " compofe a city of themfelves ; the architecture merits your attention, but you will be ftill more gratified with the extenfive view of the Apennines*, the Tyrrhenian fea, the Pontine iflands, and the capital of our empire, with innumerable leffer towns, all of which form an interefting profpect for the fanctuary of the temple †. You will obferve the Pharos for directing diftant mariners to pay a paffing falute to the throne of Fortune. A multitude of votaries crowd her fhrine, and her oracles are delivered with fufficient art to fupport the reputation of her power. You will fee, in the mofaic pavement ‡ given by Sylla, the various fcenes of life reprefented by Egyp-

* From one window of the palace this aftonifhing view is to be feen.

† Now the palace. The ancient femicircular ftaircafe ftill ferves for the entrance of this magnificent houfe, which contains a church, theatre, armoury, &c.

‡ This mofaic pavement is to be feen in the palace : it is the moft ancient known in Italy.

tian

tian figures, which he intended should denote that all depends on the fickle goddess.
You perceive the situation of Præneste: this
hill, of difficult access, has often been fatal
to its inhabitants, whose fidelity to Rome
has for ever endeared them to our nation.
The place has been frequently attacked, and
the conquerors have cruelly revenged on its
citizens the toil and difficulties which they
had undergone during the siege. The horrid
massacre committed by order of Sylla, and
the death of the younger Marius, rendered
him the solitary master of this city: he attributed his successes to Fortune; but had he
ascribed them to a higher cause, he would not
have sullied his victory by the destruction
of twelve thousand Romans and Præneftians.
Blind to his own fate, he, from that moment, sealed his guilt by assuming the ap-
pellation of THE FORTUNATE, and became
the most wretched of the human species."

Valerius, by previously acquainting the

                              Britons

Britons with the fubjects that were to claim their attention, acted in a manner very different from what is generally practifed with regard to travellers. It is cuftomary to wait till their eyes are fixed on any particular work of art or nature, and then to call off their attention by an ill-timed difplay of knowledge, which confufes their ideas, and explains away their power of obfervation. The princes were, on the contrary, prepared for the hiftorical part of the fcene, and they were not importunately difturbed from making their own reflections on the objects as they appeared to them: they were confequently left to an exertion of their judgment, and we were far from being difpleafed with the remarks which it produced.

When we returned to the villa, we found Afinius Gallus * walking with Lepidus in the portico, and relating, with a vehemence

* Annals of Tacitus, in various places, and other authors

natural

natural to him, the affair of Varilia Apuleia*. To the crimes of which she is accused, has lately been added the charge of speaking disrespectfully of the late emperor, of Tiberius, and of his mother. Asinius exclaimed loudly against the application of laws, first intended for the safety of the people, to the support of despotism in the reigning family; and inveighed, with acrimonious warmth, against the part which he supposed Tiberius would act in this affair. Lepidus answered him with coolness and moderation, saying, that he conceived Tiberius had too much understanding not to reflect, that it was as imprudent to punish discourses like those of Varilia, as it was unjustifiable to utter them. At this moment entered Messala, and the younger Valerius Maximus. My uncle, who had hitherto been silent, took occasion, from their arrival, to change the topic of conversation, and questioned Maxi-

* Tacitus, Book ii.

mus

mus on his literary purfuits. He replied, that it was his intention to compofe a volume of MEMORABLE EXAMPLES *, felected from the Roman hiftory, and from that of foreign nations, (which he would clafs under the diftinct heads of virtues and vices.

Valerius, who knows the difpofition of Maximus, applauded his defign, but admonifhed him to avoid beftowing exceffive praifes on any modern. " You would undoubtedly wifh," faid he, " that your work fhould be read and approved by pofterity; I know you too well to fufpect that you will give a falfe reprefentation of any great characters who may have been connected with an oppreffed or unfortunate party : you will do them juftice : but if you fpeak of thofe in power, with only the encomiums that may be ftrictly their due, you will, notwithftanding, be accounted a flatterer. I would

---

* This work ftill extant.

likewife

likewife counfel you againft entering into a
detail of religious ceremonies, as it is difficult to relate the circumftances which gave
rife to them, without adopting popular errors
and fabulous traditions.   Content yourfelf
with recording thofe anecdotes which may
teach our defcendants to fupport the caufe of
virtue, and to ftop the progrefs of degeneracy.   You have ftudied much; your reflections will be elegant and accurate; you will
preferve the memory of many great actions
performed by obfcure perfons, and confequently omitted by hiftorians in general; a
pleafing and, I could almoft fay, a god-like
tafk! Impartial Heaven had the fame rewards
in ftore for the faithful flave of Panopion,
who fuffered himfelf to be killed, that he
might fave the life of his profcribed mafter,
as for the illuftrious Regulus, who eternized
his name by that faith and magnanimity,
which all nations, and all ages will celebrate."

As

As you are not unacquainted, my friend, with the character of Maximus, you will easily judge which part of the instructions of Valerius he is most likely to follow.

Messala was, during this time, engaged in a dispute with Gallus, on the different merits of our modern orators. Each of them, being the son of a man celebrated for eloquence, concluded that he had an hereditary right to decide on this topic. So natural is it sometimes to suppose that the gifts of nature descend like those of fortune. Messala, who had by far the advantage in solidity of argument, was seconded by Lepidus; but their reasons could not prevail against the volubility of Asinius: he persisted in his opinion, and harangued till the ground of the question was forgotten, and till he had warmed himself sufficiently to declare, that his father * was superior to

* He wrote a book to prove it, which was refuted by the emperor Claudius.

Cicero

Cicero in every faculty that conftitutes an orator. His two opponents avoided making any reply to this declaration, which determined him to appeal to Valerius.

" As to Pollio," faid my uncle, " I ever revered his talents, and refpected his virtues ; he was the friend of my father *, and though he did not think proper to take the fame active part in the war between Anthony and Octavius, Poplicola fpoke highly of the propriety of his conduct, and confidered him as one of the few perfons who were not ungrateful to the unfortunate Triumvir. His eloquence has never been queftioned, but that of Cicero admits of no comparifon ; yet do not imagine, Afinius, that I mean to detract from the merit of your father by this affertion. Cicero lived at a time in which the commonwealth ftill exifted, though in the midft of faction and civil war:

* Poplicola, who commanded the right wing at the battle of Actium with Marc Anthony. Plutarch.

in

in thofe days muſt be dated the triumph of eloquence, a talent which owes its being to liberty, and uſually becomes deſtructive to its parent. Our republic had arrived at the ſummit of its greatneſs; every advantage which experience and learning could beſtow, was open to the man of genius; and the moſt important intereſts were to be difcuſſed before active rivals and enlightened audiences; what more is neceſſary to form an orator? Aſi-nius Pollio * retained much of the ancient perfection: his ſtyle was copious and elegant, that of Meſſala intereſting and perſuaſive: they were as much ſuperior to us, as I am afraid our followers will be inferior. It would be fruitleſs to expect, in the preſent circumſtances, the ſevere gravity of Brutus,

* For the character of theſe orators ſee Tacitus Dial. de Orat. Quintilian, &c.

The Romans were naturally eloquent, but oratory did not become a ſcience amongſt them before the end of the ſecond punic war.

Paleſtrine is ſtill famous for roſes.

the

the ſtrength and ſpirit of Cæſar, or the accumulated excellencies of Cicero. While we read their works, we may ſave from total extinction the fire which animated their boſoms; but the flame cannot burn with the ſame vehemence and luſtre; nor can we, like Prometheus, be ſupplied from the pure ſource that once enlightened, but would now conſume us. Happy were thoſe ages in which oratory was neither ſtudied nor regretted! They were the ages of the Decii, of the Fabii, of the Marcelli."

The hour of repaſt here broke in upon the converſation, and, as ſoon as this was over, Aſinius returned to his houſe at Præneſte, where he has been ſtaying ſome days with Vipſania * and his family. Meſſala and his friend ſet out for Rome by a beautiful moon-

---

* Daughter of Marcus Agrippa and Pomponia, married firſt to Tiberius, afterwards to Aſinius Gallus; it was remarked that ſhe was the only child of Agrippa who died a natural death; ſhe was the mother of Druſus.

light:

light: the Britifh princes retired to reft, and I remained with Valerius and Lepidus in a femicircular colonnade, defigned by Vitruvius * for my grandfather Poplicola, who was one of his chief patrons. It was originally ornamented with the bufts of Anacreon, Theocritus, Sappho, Alcæus, and Simonides, to which Valerius has added thofe of Virgil, Horace, and Tibullus. On the pedeftal of each is a bafs-relief alluding to their works. I was greatly pleafed with thofe of Cupid afking admittance at the door of Anacreon, Danäe expofed on the billows with her child, the doves covering the infant Horace with leaves of myrtle and laurel, Delia weeping over the urn of her lover, and Gallus complaining of the cruel Lycoris to Apollo, and the Sylvan deities. This elegant building is open to a large extent of garden, perfumed by a variety of flowers, and particularly of

* The celebrated architeft lived in the time of Julius Cæfar and Auguftus.

rofes,

rofes, with which this country abounds at all feafons of the year.

It was here that Poplicola chiefly refided, after Auguftus became mafter of the empire; and from this place the poet Horace addreffed to the elder Lollius his epiftle * on the moral leffons to be found in Homer.   Near the fpot where now ftands his buft, he ufed to inftruct my mother, when a child, to repeat with accuracy and grace the fecular ode †, in the performance of which fhe was eminently diftinguifhed.

After we were left to ourfelves, Lepidus declared it was very aftonifhing to hear Afinius declaim fo violently againft the emperor in private focieties, whilft he often gave his vote in compliance with the moft extravagant demands of power, obferving that he had neither the merit of· firmnefs,

* Book i. Epiftle 2.

† The fecular games were celebrated in the year of Rome 737.

nor the circumfpection of prudence, and that
·probably he would fall an unpitied facrifice
to his own duplicity.

" I agree with you," anfwered Valerius,
" as to the imprudence of his conduct, but
I believe it proceeds merely from temerity
and ambition. He diflikes Tiberius, but he
wifhes to retain the influence acquired by
his connexion with the Cæfarian family,
I remember * that when Auguftus, a. fhort
time before his death, was giving his opinion
of the leading characters in the fenate, he
faid that you, Lepidus, had the talents and
qualifications neceffary to render yourfelf
mafter of the empire, but added, that you
would difdain thus to profit by. them. His
judgment of Afinius Gallus was directly
oppofite; he believed him defirous of becoming the ruler of his country, but unequal
to the arduous tafk of obtaining fuch an ele-

* Tacitus, Book 1.

vated

vated ſtation.   Your moderation has always kept you no leſs diſtant from petulant oppoſition, than from mean ſervility. You are therefore reſpected and honoured by the reigning prince, though your anceſtor was the rival of Auguſtus, and your father his victim. On the contrary, I believe there is not a man exiſting to whom Tiberius has a greater averſion than to Gallus. He never forgave him for marrying Vipſania after he himſelf had divorced her in compliance with the requeſt of Auguſtus. I know not whether you were informed of a circumſtance which happened during your abſence from Italy : he met her by accident, and ſo much diſorder was viſible in his countenance, that ſhe was enjoined to avoid, for the future, all places where Tiberius might appear.   Unhappy with Julia, miſtruſtful of all who ſurrounded him, he regretted being deprived of the only perſon to whom he had a real attachment ; even now, he is wretched whenever Druſus frequents the

Q 2

houſe

houfe of Afinius, though he cannot, with any propriety, deny him the permiffion of vifiting a mother whom he tenderly loves.

I was affected, my friend, with what I heard relative to the affection of Tiberius for Vipfania ; it was the firft time I had ever felt for him a fentiment of pity. Who knows, thought I, how much his difpofition may have been changed by a proceeding unworthy of Auguftus ? But a moment's reflection told me that Tiberius had no right to complain when he would meanly fubmit to fuch a requeft. I could not refrain from exclaiming, " How different was the con-duct of Julius Cæfar, whom all the menaces of Sylla could not induce to break the union he had formed with a daughter of the cruel dictator's greateft enemy !"

Valerius finiled at the warmth with which I fpoke, and told me, he was well affured that no confideration would ever prevail with me to facrifice my affections to fear or am-bition,

bition: "I know not of any motive," added he, which can authorize an action of this nature: whatever is in itself wrong and difgraceful, is not to be juftified even by the plea of neceffity."

"I am very fenfible of his diflike to all intercourfe with the houfe of Gallus," interrupted Lepidus, "but I always attributed it to the pride inherent for fo many ages in the Claudian family: I concluded that Tiberius wifhed to obliterate, as far as poffible, every remembrance of his connexion with Vipfania; who, though a daughter of the great Agrippa, was fuppofed to degrade the family images by introducing amongft them that of Pomponius Atticus, a Roman knight, who never enjoyed any dignities in the republic. It muft be owned that great and important fervices have been rendered to the ftate by the numerous heroes of the Claudian race; but the Decemvir Appius; the haughty dame who wifhed her brother had loft more

Q 3

citizens

citizens from the commonwealth, that she might not have been incommoded with a crowd; and the supercilious obstinacy with which even the best of the Claudii always fomented the disputes between the patricians and plebeians, are all melancholy examples, and fatal prognostics, which have been neglected till too late ! How different was the character of the Julian race! And how certain this truth, that winning affability establishes dominion, and lofty despotism takes advantage of it !"

Lepidus now withdrew, and Valerius, having staid a few minutes longer, gave me every reason to hope that he would soon gratify my fondest wishes. After he left me, I found it impossible to compose myself to rest; my heart and my imagination were fully employed ; I wandered into the gardens, and, invited by the soft lustre of the moon, directed my steps towards a long avenue of elms, which decorate the plantations.

tions.   I had scarcely entered the walk when I observed a person who retreated at my approach: this engaged me to follow, and by the stature and gait it appeared to be Drusus.   You will conceive my agitation; I pursued him in haste, but he took a different path, and was lost to my sight.   I spent the greatest part of the night in fruitless search; and this morning I went to the house of Afinius to enquire for him, when I was told that he had been there, but was then on his way to Rome.   I immediately hastened our departure, having first interrogated the servants of Valerius, whether they knew that Drusus had been at Præneste.   They reported that he had been seen by several of them in the gardens, which are open to all; but that he had not expressed any desire to visit their master.

On my arrival here, I went to the palace where he was said to be hourly expected, but not yet arrived; and that probably he had

Q 4

taken

taken the road of Tusculum. You have no idea, my friend, of my embarrassment. Happily Valerius returns 'to-morrow, and it is impossible that Drusus can for ever escape me.

I AM aftonifhed and deeply affected, my friend, at what I have heard fince clofing my laft letter; my apprehenfions are dreadful, my indignation is beyond expreffion; I have fcarcely fortitude to relate what has paffed.

No fooner did I hear that Valerius was returned from Prænefte, than I went to his houfe, and found him engaged with many of his friends. Having obtained permiffion to vifit his lovely daughter, I flew to her apartment elated with joy and tendernefs. She was in tears, and had not power to welcome me: you will conceive how much I was alarmed: I entreated her to difclofe the caufe of this affliction, which furprifed and terrified me, at a time when all confpired to

diffufe

diffuse satisfaction and transport around us. She desired me to follow her into the garden, where, as soon as we were at some distance from her attendants, she shewed me a letter which she had received from Drusus on her arrival in town.

After the warmest declarations of a passion, which he professes to have combated and concealed since the first moment he saw her, because he was sensible of the obstacles that opposed his happiness, he declares that he is now resolved to be divorced from Livia, and has not only the consent, but the approbation of Tiberius to offer his hand to Valeria. He requests permission to see her; complains that he has often attempted it in vain while at Præneste; and promises to explain whatever may have the appearance of precipation or indelicacy in his conduct. He conjures her not to reject a proposal on which depends the fate of one far dearer to her than herself; and concludes by assuring

her

her that his entreaties are dictated, not more by his ardent affection for her, than by his profound and constant veneration for her father.

After I had read the letter, Valeria asked me with a faltering voice what I thought of the contents : I was incapable of returning an answer : a chilly horror glided through my veins ; and the fatal mystery disclosed itself to my indignant imagination with all the strength of conviction. I remained silent, and revolved in my agitated mind the various consequences that might attend any sudden determination. Valeria trembled, and looked on me with inexpressible concern. " Marcus !" said she, " this silence is more painful than words of the most fatal import ; think in what a dreadful state of suspense I have passed the moments since my receiving this letter. Assist me, guide me through the dreary labyrinth in which I am involved—I cannot support that look of despair."

It

It is not defpair, anfwered I; it is refentment—it is fury. I have from the firft been
jealous of fome finifter defigr.s in Drufus,
but did not expect this dreadful difcovery,
and that he would have ufed menaces for
the accomplifhment of his wifhes—Give me
the letter—I will feek this detefted difturber
of our felicity—I will cancel in his blood
thofe obligations on which he fets fo immenfe a value.

Thefe, or fimilar expreffions, were fuggefted to me by the momentary madnefs
which had feized me. Valeria turned pale,
and, with a voice that might have foothed the
anger of a favage, entreated me to calm myfelf:
fhe faid the paffion with which I was tranfported made me incapable of reflection;
that, when I refumed my ufual tranquillity, I
might perhaps difcover that Drufus had
been conftrained to act in this manner, and
that we might be unjuft in fuppofing him fo
guilty as he appeared. This obfervation,

far

far from appeafing, added fuel to my rage:
a kind of momentary frenzy fuggefted to
me that Valeria might feek to excufe Drufus
from motives of partiality—I know not what
I faid—my fenfes were difordered; and I
did not recover myfelf till I perceived that,
overcome by anguifh, fhe had funk fainting
on the border of a fountain near which we
ftood. It was fome time before fhe revived:
and I then conjured her to pardon the violence into which I had been betrayed by
excefs of affliction.

" Alas!" faid Valeria, " my apprehenfions
have taken from me the power of explaining
what I wifh, or what I fear; I would have
you fpeak to Drufus, engage him to acknowledge whether it is by an abfolute order of
the emperor, that he has written to me this
fatal letter, or whether any choice is left me
befide the dreadful alternative of committing
parricide, or pronouncing vows which my
heart can never juftify. O Marcus! if

eternal

eternal feclufion from the world; if to bid
farewell to my father, and to you, would
fatisfy the cruelty of our enemies, and fave
me from a crime, I would complete the facrifice—but I fear it would be of no avail—
All I entreat of you at prefent, is, to rife fuperior to your paffions, and not to fuffer a deftructive though juft indignation prevent you from
taking the only meafure through which I can
perceive a ray of hope. Speak calmly to
Drufus: tell him that I efteem his virtues,
and would fave him from lafting ftings of
felf-reproach; when reflection, too late, convinces him that by one act of tyranny he
forfeits the friendfhip of Germanicus, de-
grades the facred honour of his family, and
configns Valeria to perpetual mifery. He
will then be fenfible of his error, and will
prevent its dreadful confequences; he will
liften to your admonitions: but your menaces
could only end in the extinction of every
hope that now fupports me. Promife me

you

you will reftrain your anger—I have no truft but in yourfelf—I am not accuftomed to act without the advice of a father: this is the firft event I have ever concealed from his knowledge: twice was I on the point of difclofing the fatal fecret, when, happily, my reafon interpofed, and reminded me that perhaps we may owe his prefervation to his being for ever ignorant of the fhameful propofal."

I could not difobey the commands of Valeria, promifing to fupprefs my emotions, and left her that I might go in fearch of Drufus; but he was in the apartment of Germanicus, a place at this time ill fuited to our meeting. I did not enter, as it would have been impoffible for me to conceal my agitation; and I have ftill fome expectation of bringing him to a fenfe of honour, without divulging a circumftance which muft for ever difturb the quiet of the Cæfarian family. I have defired that Drufus may be acquainted how earneftly I wifh to

fpeak

ſpeak with him alone. Farewell, Septimius; I am once more going in ſearch of him; but, whatever may be the conſequences of our meeting, be aſſured that my affection for Valeria, however ardent, is not the only cauſe of my indignation againſt him. I cannot blame him for being ſenſible of her perfections, though I would contend for the poſſeſſion of them againſt the univerſe; nor will I relinquiſh them while I have life: but the diſhonourable manner in which it appears he would obtain her, is repugnant to every principle and duty, that we hold ſacred among mankind.

IMMERSED in the gulph of mifery, it is with difficulty, my friend, that I can collect my wandering fpirits to communicate to you the horrors of our fate. I yefterday bade you adieu, in the intention of feeking Drufus; I found he waited for my return; he was alone, and we retired to the remoteft apartment. I reprefented to him, with fufficient calmnefs, the refpect which the dignity and virtues of Valerius had a right to command; I repeated to him the injunctions of Valeria, and required a full explanation of the letter which had raifed her alarms and excited my refentment.

Drufus at firft endeavoured to palliate the

Vol. II.   R   expreffions

expreffions he had ufed, and affirmed that he had long been attached to Valeria.

" Is it furprifing," faid he, " that I fhould wifh, by an union with the moft amiable of her fex, to fecure my own happinefs, and free myfelf from a connexion with Livia, who has neither a regard for me nor for Germanicus. He is too juft, and too fenfible of the mifconduct of his fifter to refent a ftep which would be conducive to the general tranquillity of our family. Livia was never my choice; the will of Auguftus directed our union; and after the firft emotion of offended pride has fubfided, fhe will rejoice to be fet at liberty from an alliance of which fhe has never known the value, nor practifed the duties."

I remonftrated with your friend on the impoffibility of his obtaining the confent of Valeria, or of her father. " You will perhaps," faid I, " confider my remonftrance as interefted; and I frankly confefs that I love

Valeria

Valeria beyond every other confideration except my honour; but it is that, and not my paffion, which now fpeaks.   Think not that ever I will permit you to receive her hand; you have rendered yourfelf unworthy of it by the infidious means you employed for obtaining intelligence of the place of my uncle's retreat; by your unfolicited inter- ference in the concerns of our family; by your myfterious conduct throughout the whole of this proceeding; and, laftly, by the fhameful advantage you have taken of your influence with Tiberius, in feeking to inti- midate a daughter, whofe tendernefs and piety might lead her to sacrifice her own peace of mind to the fafety of her father. Reflect on the unmanly part you have acted: recal to mind the honourable principles of your anceftors; fhew yourfelf worthy of the name of Drufus; for that of Cæfar has been made subfervient to the purpofes of def- potifm.   Caft off the borrowed majefty

R 2

which

which cannot make you formidable to men
who fet no value on their lives, but as they
are ufeful to the republic; and forbear to
blaft the growing virtues, which may render
you dear to Rome, by an action only becoming a Tarquin."

Drufus remained fome moments filent: at
length he rofe haftily, and taking me by the
hand, "Marcus!" faid he with emotion, "I
am guilty, and I confefs my guilt; educated
amidft flatterers and flaves, I have known no
bounds to my will; and as I could not obtain
your confidence, I employed unworthy means
to be informed of the place to which Valerius was exiled; but I fwear to all the immortal Gods, that my intentions were honourable and difinterefted. You will not
fuppofe that fear can fway the heart of Drufus; I avow my fault, in order to clear myfelf from the other afperfions you have
thrown on me. Hear me patiently, and
then indulge your refentment; I will not

fay

say but my love for Valeria might influence my zeal for her father's return; but I did not then hope for her hand as the reward of my fuccefs. I wifhed indeed that fhe might owe his deliverance to me: the reft I left to time and to herfelf. I made ufe of every argument that might engage my father to comply with my requeft for the recal of Valerius; I pleaded your fervices, and the unvaried tenor of your uncle's conduct, the love and veneration of his fellow-citizens, and the odium to which the emperor would be expofed if he refufed reftoring him to Rome. At length Tiberius yielded to my earneft requeft; but it was on a condition which I accepted not without a fenfe of the difficulties I fhould experience, and of the want of generofity with which I fhould be accufed. But reflect on my fituation— ' Drufus,' faid the emperor, ' I am not unacquainted with your fentiments for Valeria; you are incited by fomething more than

R 3

refpect

refpect for her father, to folicit his recal: I confent to your defire, on condition you perfuade Valeria to become your wife. This alliance can alone remove the apprehenfions which the extenfive influence of Titus Valerius, and the inftability of human fortune, create in my mind. I have more reafons for what I now urge than it is neceffary to communicate to you: it is enough that you are informed the fafety of this empire, and of the Julian family, depends on our fecuring, or annihilating the over-grown power of the man, whom you imprudently wifh to reftore to the fenate. I will give orders that he fhall be conducted hither in a manner fuitable to his dignity, and I will neglect no means to conciliate his friendfhip; and if you fucceed in perfuading his daughter to fuch an union, a tafk which furely cannot be difficult to the fon of Tiberius, my fears will be ended, and I fhall even be led to approve the temerity of that conduct, which

has

has had such fortunate issue. But should these designs be ineffectual, I must inform you that Valerius and your father cannot exist at one time : my resolves are unalterable, therefore you have no time to lose.   Your proceeding has constrained me to act in a manner that leaves you no alternative but to consult your own inclinations, and promote the interest of your family, or to destroy the person whom you wish to save. It shall be my care to satisfy Germanicus and Livia."

" Can you blame me, Marcus," continued the prince, " if I had not the magnanimity, or rather the cruelty, to refuse this offered blessing ? I was convinced that Valeria would revolt from my proposal, unless her father supported it by his counsel and authority ; I knew he would reject it with scorn, if he were acquainted with the terms on which Tiberius permitted me to make it ; and I had no room to hope that he would listen to my suit, except he had reason to imagine

R 4

that

that Valeria's inclinations correfponded with mine. I knew not any means that could induce her to ufe her intereft with her father, except by infinuating that his future fate depended on her compliance; for I durft not hope, what would have been my firft wifh, to owe this ineftimable bleffing to her favourable fentiments for me."

You may imagine, my deareft friend, the confternation with which I liftened to the dif-courfe of Drufus; I here interrupted him with exclamations againft the tyranny of Tiberius, and the unjuft fufpicions which he pre-tended to entertain of Valerius. I was over-whelmed with the dreadful truth of which I had always formed fome vague conjectures, but from which my mind had recoiled with horror. I muft, however, do your friend the juftice to fay, that he appeared confcious of his fault, and deeply afflicted with the fatal confequences that muft enfue from it; but he ftill entreated that I would prevail on
Valeria

Valeria to accept his propofal, and that I would be the advocate of his paffion.

O Septimius! I am ready to meet tortures and death to preferve Valerius; nay more—I feel that I have fortitude for a feverer trial——; but never, never will Valerius confent to fo difhonourable an alliance! Had we the power of difguifing our looks and actions, were our fentiments to be for ever concealed from his paternal penetration, his own wifdom would tell him that Tiberius did not approve of the propofal but from interefted and unworthy views. No; he will never yield to a propofal fo repugnant to his principles: he is loft; and the diffembling tyrant, with a refinement of cruelty peculiar to himfelf, would make his children ftrike the blow that is to deftroy him! How can I inform Valeria of the fatal converfation that has paffed between myfelf and Drufus! How can I meet the eyes of that great, that venerated man, whom I will

not

not, whom I cannot furvive!—My friend, never till now was I acquainted with real misfortune; all other forrows might be endured with fortitude, but this furpaffes the ftrength of human reafon.

IT is matter of furprife to me, Septimius, that I ftill retain the ufe of my fenfes; and had I wholly loft them, I fhould be far lefs wretched. I have been with Valeria; her terrors and afflictions have preyed on her health, and the malice of Tiberius may foon be doubly fatiated. Alarmed at the illnefs of his daughter, Valerius never leaves her; and her eyes are in vain directed to me for confolation. I dare not, even by a look, give hopes that may encourage and deceive her: a mournful filence reigns in the apartment; defpair and anxiety are painted by turns on her beauteous, though languid, countenance; and the tender cares of her father encreafe her fufferings.

I know

I know not how to fupport the melancholy fcene; and cannot behold Valerius without reflecting that a few days, nay, a few hours, may for ever deprive me of this ineftimable parent, and plunge Valeria into the abyfs of wretchednefs! Her father obferves my affliction; he attributes it folely to my concern for his daughter; but feeks in vain to account for the fource of her apparent diftrefs, while our mutual fufferings are inexpreffibly increafed by the impoffibility of giving vent to our feelings, and by the neceffity of difguifing our fentiments from Valerius.

I write to you from his apartment, where I am retired from the torment of conftraint, and where I can open my heart to Septimius. O! my friend, bear with the incoherent expreffions of my defpair; receive them as proofs of my friendfhip and confidence: I have not power to anfwer the various expoftulations of your letters; but

your

your goodnefs is engraved deeply on my heart, and can only be effaced with life. Your meffenger waits, and I muft clofe the packet: farewell! my dear Septimius! Heaven knows if we fhall meet again! Is it poffible that I can live with honour, and not revenge Valerius? Has not my return precipitated his fate?

I learn that Drufus is at this moment with Valerius; what will be the refult of their converfation? I muft take this opportunity of acquainting the unhappy Valeria with what paffed yefterday between Drufus and myfelf. It is neceffary fhe fhould know it, and yet how do I dread to give her the information.

LETTER

I RESUME the melancholy history of our fate, which seems suspended for a moment; but our present situation is like the gloomy calm that intervenes between the bursts of thunder in a storm. If my memory does not fail me, when I last wrote, I mentioned that Drusus was engaged in private conference with Valerius, and that I had summoned all my remaining resolution to destroy, at one dreadful interview, the last hopes of his unhappy daughter.

She soon read the fatal intelligence in my countenance, and assured me she was prepared for the worst I had to relate. I repeated every thing that had passed; my heart was full; I could not forbear expressions of

my

my unbounded tendernefs, and vain complaints of the hopes, which my heart had
fondly cherifhed, of finding in her the reward of all my fufferings. The lovely maid
heard and fhared in my anguifh; our tears
flowed in a mingled flream; we were both
ready to facrifice our mutual happinefs for
the fafety of Valerius; we confirmed each
other in our refolution; but how, and in
what manner, could we conceal within our
bofoms the caufe by which we were compelled to fo cruel a facrifice?

"If Drufus," faid Valeria, "fhould perfuade my father to confent to this fatal
alliance, I will, I muft acquiefce—but
then—to counterfeit the fentiments of my
heart, to deceive Valerius with a feigned
attachment to the fon of his murderer.
Marcus! it is impoffible—we may perifh
with him, but we cannot fave him."

At this moment Valerius entered, he took

his

his place near Valeria; neither of us durſt enquire what had been the object of the viſit of Druſus: he remained ſome time ſilent, and looked upon us both with ſuch inexpreſſible affection, that by an involuntary motion we fell on our knees before him, and bathed his hands with our tears.

"My children!" ſaid he, "riſe and hear what your father requeſts from your filial piety: life is ever uncertain to all, and more eſpecially to the man who loves his country, and ſupports her laws, at a time when many are intereſted in their deſtruction. Next to Rome, you are the objects of my care; let me then be aſſured of your future happineſs, and enjoy the conſolation of ſeeing you joined by indiſſoluble bonds. I have long-read the hearts of Marcus and Valeria; I ſee they are firmly united. When I imagined that fate had deprived me of Marcus, I knew not where to find another worthy of Valeria:

you

you were formed for each other, and all a father's hopes are excited by your mutual affection."

We attempted to speak, but had not power to reply, and our faltering words confirmed Valerius in the truth of his sentiments.

" My children," said he, resuming his discourse, " you wish to conceal from me a secret of which it is necessary I should be informed ; your attempts to disguise it any longer are in vain : Drusus has been with me, and has demanded Valeria in marriage. The pertubation of mind, which has been visible in you both, convinces me that you are acquainted with this proposal, and that you suppose my safety depends on the acceptance of an alliance, which Tiberius would not have desired without interested views. I will not upbraid you with an error which had its source in your affection to me, but you are to remember that it is

VOL. II.   S   the

the honour, and not the safety of Valerius
which you are now to consult, if your regard
for me is such as I wish, and believe it to be.
You should not, Marcus, suffer yourself to
be so far blinded by anxiety for my personal
safety, as not to feel that nothing could
justify so dishonourable a contract, not
though it could have been possible to keep
me for ever ignorant of the motives. I have
not communicated my thoughts to Drusus;
for I would not wish to humiliate him
by any unnecessary declaration of my suspicions: I attribute his conduct merely to
imprudence, and to that want of delicacy,
which often is the result of too exalted, as
well as too ignoble a station. I have refused
to bestow on him my daughter, assuring him
that I always intended her for Marcus:
he used many arguments to shake my resolution, but I evidently perceived that he was
ashamed of the part he has been acting. I
desire

defire that no enmity may fubfift between him and you : his intentions were lefs guilty than they appeared.

" Difquiet not yourfelves, my children, I fhall await with compofure the decifions of Tiberius, or the defigns of thofe who may think it their intereft to remove me from Rome.   I fhall frequent the fenate, and vifit my friends as ufual, but fhall go unarmed.   I am not carelefs of life: my domeftic enjoyments are perfectly conformable to my hopes, and the efteem of my fellow-citizens gives me reafon to fuppofe that my zeal for my country has not been without notice; but it is impoffible to guard againft the arts of treachery, and it is incompatible with my duty to avoid them.   I muft not fee you thus alarmed for my fake: threats are often without effect, and the malice of our enemies is fometimes defeated by the unforefeen interpofition of Providence, when human care would be of no avail."

S 2   Encouraged

Encouraged by the firmnefs of Valerius, I related to him every circumftance that had come to our knowledge, and we fhewed him the letter of Drufus. He liftened calmly to our narration, and then continued to compofe our minds by various reafons tending to prove that our apprehenfions had not fufficient foundation, or to arm us againft whatever might happen.

Drufus came the next day, and informed me that he was ordered * by Tiberius immediately to join the Illyrian army. He exprefled great contrition for the uneafinefs he had given us, and aflured me he had faid all in his power to convince the emperor that he would wrong Valerius to imagine him his enemy. Drufus did not afk to fee Valeria, but took leave of my uncle with fuch apparent forrow and refpect, as feemed to indicate his fufpicions that the refolutions of

* Tacitus, Book 2.

Tiberius

Tiberius were unalterable. Notwithstanding these appearances, and the distrust which hangs over me, I am sometimes disposed to yield to the constant admonitions of Valerius. I am ashamed to testify my fears in his presence: his virtue awes me into silence, and I would willingly believe that no wretch can be sufficiently base to lift a sacrilegious hand against him.

Valeria has recovered her health, but not her former serenity; whenever her father is detained by public or private concerns beyond her expectation, she relapses into all the anxieties that first affected her. Why am I forbid by duty from destroying with one blow the cause of all our miseries, or perishing in the attempt!

Germanicus, who had long perceived a coolness between Livia and Drusus, has seriously admonished his sister to reform her conduct, and use every endeavour to regain the

S 3

confidence

confidence of her hufband. Whether it be from inclination or from fufpicion of what has paffed, fhe has, however, attended to his counfels, and defired permiffion to follow Drufus into Illyria.   He is this morning departed, and Germanicus will foon fet out for his province, whither Agrippina accompanies him. The emperor is impatient to be alone : the prefence of his fons alarms his jealous fears: a gloomy difcontent is brooding in his mind, and the flighteft circumftances give him umbrage. The pufillanimous wretch who lives in the continual dread of danger to himfelf is capable of every crime, and his torments increafe as he plunges deeper into cruelty. My heart fwells with indignation when I think that the brave and honeft man may fall a victim to the coward and the artful. Valerius, undaunted in the midft of peril, and fuperior to all the malice or treachery of mankind, infpires me with the fame heroifm which animates his breaft.

breaſt : often I reproach myſelf for diſ-
truſting the protection of Heaven in ſo juſt
a cauſe, and perſuade myſelf that Tiberius
and his worthleſs miniſters have not power
to hurt him.

THIS morning, my friend, the contract was signed between Valeria and myself. Nothing could equal my felicity, if I were assured of the safety of our father; for such I love to call him. That part of his time which is not devoted to public businefs, is wholly confecrated to us: he paffes hours in giving me ufeful leffons for the future conduct of my life, and inculcates every precept that can teach me to diftinguifh myfelf in the fervice of my country. He has taken the neceffary fteps for my advancement in the army, and has added another eftate in the Sabine territories to that which Sigifmar inhabits at Tibur. He omits nothing that can contribute to our fatisfaction; but do not

thefe

thefe cares imply that he expects to leave us? This dreadful idea embitters all my happiness.

. The day is fixed for our marriage; but a melancholy foreboding feems to tell me that one fatal moment may blaft my approaching joys. O! Septimius, I fhould be too greatly bleft if thefe terrors were not continually before me: I am not eafy whenever I part from Valerius; whether in the fenate or the forum I would ftill be near him. His friends appear to have caught the infection of my fears; they are always in crowds around him; or, perhaps, I attribute to them my fentiments, when they only feek his fociety from motives of affection, or defire to profit by his counfels.

The German legates are departed *, having received for anfwer, that as their fovereigns never affifted the Romans, when at

* Tacitus, Book 2.

war

war with the common enemy, no fuccours will be granted them againft Arminius; but it has been promifed, that Drufus fhall here-after be fent as a mediator to eftablifh peace between them. I have written a few lines to communicate this pleafing intelligence to Sigifmar, now Titus Valerius; and have at the fame time acquainted him with his being enrolled in the equeftrian order.

I have felt the utmoft concern at parting from Germanicus: he paffes through Illyria, to fee his brother, and from thence will vifit the moft remarkable cities of Greece in his way to Syria. He leaves Rome with un-ufual regret; but is ill qualified by his frank and generous difpofition to withftand the malicious artifice of Pifo. "My friend," faid he, "I am neither going to acquire glory, nor to oppofe manly enemies: you have feen me undifmayed in the moft perilous engagements, but I feel at prefent a repug-nance which I attempt in vain to conquer;

I cannot

I cannot approve the origin of thefe troubles in the eaft: they arife from the vindictive temper of Tiberius, who could not, when a fovereign, forget the neglect he had experienced as a private citizen. You have heard that Archelaus fell a victim to his want of refpect for the future emperor, when retired at Rhodes: his country muft now be punifhed for this offence, and for the feditions excited by the difpofal of the kingdom. Thefe unwarlike nations will give me no additional glory, and all my actions will be mifinterpreted or calumniated by Pifo. How far his malice may extend is beyond my apprehenfion; but I would wifh that the defires of my enemies might not be gratified till I had formed the tender minds of my children to the love of virtue and their country; for I cannot fupport the thought that misfortunes or profperity fhould ever make them unworthy of their birth, or of

the

the love which their fellow citizens already testify to them and to their father."

Being here interrupted by the arrival of many of his friends, he changed the subject of converfation; and indeed it was the first time I ever heard him exprefs a difapprobation of the meafures of Tiberius, or complain of his own fituation. I know not whether I muft attribute every gloomy idea to my prefent ftate of mind, but when I parted from him, my too feeling heart feemed to portend that we fhould never meet again. My feet fcarcely quitted the door of his apartment, when I wifhed to return, and bid him once more farewell; but I reproached myfelf with fuperftitious weaknefs, and flowly left the manfion of my beloved friend and valiant leader.

Another circumftance which increafes my uneafinefs is, that the treacherous Philocles has remained at Rome, and is frequently

feen

seen at the palace: like an evil genius he haunts the dwellings of the great, foments their vices, and becomes the minister of their injustice. Tiberius, it is said, delights in his literary talents: the wilds of fiction engage his attention, and make him for some moments forget that he is the unhappy master of the world.

He has lately enfranchised one of his slaves, named Phædrus, who writes moral fables*, in imitation of those of Esop, with great simplicity and purity of language. Tiberius therefore knows the value of freedom, since he makes it the reward of liberal sentiments, and yet he dares to call that man his enemy who adheres to the honourable principles transmitted through a line of heroes.

I have warned the British princes against

---

* These fables are still extant.

forming

forming any connexion with the dangerous Greek; it is the only fervice I have been capable of rendering them fince my mind has been thrown into this cruel agitation.

LET-

I HAVE matters of so much importance to relate, such awful events to communicate to you, my friend, that I dispatch a messenger on purpose to inform you of all that has passed since the date of my last letter: this attention is justly due to your invariable friendship.

As I was engaged in conversation with Valerius on the day following the departure of Germanicus, and lamented with him the absence of a hero who seems formed to justify the affection of the Roman people, Cornelius Dolabella enquired for me, and, with a pale and altered countenance, entreated that I would immediately accompany him to his house. " A sudden illness," said he," " has seized Aurelia: death hovers over

her,

her, and she has conjured me not to lose a moment in conducting you to her presence—some important secret agitates her mind, and adds terrors to the fatal malady.

I wanted no further incitement, but instantly followed him with anxiety and perturbation. Though my passion for Aurelia had long since been effaced, I felt much for her melancholy situation, and entered with trembling steps the apartment to which Dolabella conducted me. It is not possible to tell how deeply I was affected when I beheld the livid paleness that disfigured her beauteous face: she bade me welcome with a troubled voice, and desired both Dolabella and myself to approach nearer to her couch: we obeyed in silence, when, ordering her women, and the physician Celsus, to withdraw, "Marcus Flaminius," said she, " I have sent for you to supplicate your forgiveness, and I know too well your generosity not to be assured that you will grant me

this

this requeſt, and likewiſe obtain for me the forgiveneſs of Dolabella. I have much to ſay, and I know not whether I ſhall have ſtrength to acquit myſelf of the painful taſk; a mortal poiſon flows in my veins—I feel its effects, and muſt be brief."

Nothing can exceed the horror with which we were ſeized : we conjured her to ſuſpend her narrative, and take ſuch remedies as might yet ſave her; but ſhe interrupted us abruptly, and, declaring that the power of art could not avail, proceeded nearly in theſe words, ſo far as the troubled ſtate of my mind allowed me to collect them.

" I am conſcious," continued ſhe, "of the errors into which I have fallen; actuated by ſelf-love, I neither ſuffered reflection nor ſenſibility to diſturb my peace : early in life I had adopted the maxim of being ſuperior to my ſex, by ſecuring my heart from the impreſſions of love, and my mind from the uſual prejudices of women. I was ſenſible

of the reprehenfion and inconveniences to
which fuch a character would expofe me,
and therefore concealed it with all the artifice
of which I was miftrefs.   I doubt not,
Marcus, you confidered my love to you
as real, which, indeed, you had every reafon to fuppofe ; but the preference with
which I diftinguifhed you, was owing to
your behaviour on your firft campaign ; to
the approbation of Rome in general, and to
the advantages you poffeffed above your
equals in rank, or in age.   My pride was
flattered by your paffion, and I faw with
pleafure your departure for Germany, in the
idea, which has fince been realifed, that you
would acquire new glory, and that the object of your choice might one day become
the moft diftinguifhed woman in her country.   When the news of the defeat of Varus,
and of the deftruction of his army, arrived
at Rome, I was not infenfible of the difap-
pointment ; my ambition felt the blow, and
I looked

I looked round with mortification on those whom I had rejected as your inferiors. Cornelius Dolabella was the most eminent of your rivals; his merits obtained universal applause, and I chose him with all that coolness and reflection which parental authority might have dictated. My parents were too indulgent not to acquiesce in my choice, and had too much confidence in my prudence, not to suffer their inclinations to be directed by mine. When you returned, covered with laurels, I felt a disquietude not to be described; I sometimes regretted that you had survived the engagement of Teutoburgium, as your subsequent honours, which surpassed even my expectation, could no longer be communicated to me; and much oftener I lamented that precipitation with which I had made a second election. You are sensible that I essayed every art imaginable to regain your affection, though your generosity would have concealed it from

T 2   Dolabella:

Dolabella: all that has paft will foon be indifferent to me, and it is but juft that you
fhould both be acquainted with the truth.
After the humiliating fcene that paffed in
the gardens of the Palatine, a humiliation
which I felt the more feverely from your
delicacy on that occafion, I loft all patience;
my mind was in perpetual agitation; I forefaw that if you difcovered the retreat of Valerius, you would undoubtedly be captivated
by the graces and virtues of Valeria. Her
filial affection to her father, and the
exceffive affliction that fhe had felt on the
death of a mother, whom fhe moft tenderly
revered, convinced me that fhe had a heart
capable of feeling and anfwering the fenfibility of yours. I then, for the firft time, repented that artificial conduct by which my
life had been directed, and yet I had recourfe
to new artifices for the prevention of what
I feared: I poffeffed a great fhare in the
confidence of Livia, and confequently muft
have

have some intercourse with Sejanus. It is true, I always entertained for him the contempt he merits, but his influence with Tiberius made it neceſſary that I ſhould avoid openly offending him: on this occaſion I communicated to the favourite my thoughts, that nothing could induce you to relinquiſh the ſearch you were about to undertake, till you had ſuccceded in the diſcovery of Valerius. He naturally feared the return of your uncle, and knew no means of preventing it without raiſing ſuſpicion. As the admiration of Druſus for Valeria, had long been no ſecret to Sejanus and myſelf, we agreed that I ſhould perſuade him to recommend to you, by the intervention of Germanicus, the Sicilian ſlave, by whoſe means he might be informed of all your proceedings. Druſus, whoſe impetuous and imprudent character is ever open even to the deſigns of his enemies, is ſtill more eaſily influenced by any woman who has the ad-

vantages

vantages of perfon and underftanding. He liftened attentively to my infinuations; and though he was at firft difgufted with the propofal of placing a flave near you to betray your meafures, he at length was moved by the apprehenfions, which I induftrioufly encouraged, that Sejanus, for whom he has the utmoft deteftation, might prevent the return of Valerius, if he did not anticipate your application, and fecure the confent of Tiberius to the reftoration of your uncle, before Sejanus could be informed that you had difcovered the place of his exile. This confideration, and a wifh that Valeria might be indebted to him for the return of her father, conquered every fcruple; and he determined to make ufe of the flave in cafe you declined to confide in his friendfhip, and to give him the early intelligence he required."

The wretched Aurelia was here conftrained to paufe by tortures, the effects of which I

fhuddered

fhuddered to behold; at length fhe recovered herfelf, and proceeded:

" The mifguided Drufus had not the flighteft fufpicion that I acted in concert with Sejanus; on the contrary, he believed that I wifhed to counteract his fchemes, and obviate their malignity *. Sejanus from motives of ambition, has long paid his court to Livia, and fhe has had the weaknefs to fhew a partiality for him which emboldens him to every attempt: I propofed, and he readily adopted the plan of perfuading the emperor to lay before his fon, when he came to folicit the return of Valerius, the alternative of an union with Valeria, or the deftruction of her father. Sejanus hoped by the divorce of Livia to obtain her for himfelf, and thus form a folid bafis for his exaltation, by an alliance with the family of his fovereign. He made a merit with the emperor

* Tacitus, Book 4.

T 4

of

of having inveſtigated the deſigns of Druſus, and found means to increaſe his fears of Valerius by repreſentations of the vindictive ſteps he might purſue, if not prevented by being ſecured firmly to the intereſt of the court. Tiberius was the more willing to put ſuch advice in execution, as he concluded it muſt certainly ſow diſcord between Druſus and Germanicus, whoſe unſhaken friendſhip is to him a ſource of conſtant uneaſineſs. Thus did the ruling paſſions of all the perſons, concerned in this tranſaction, induce them to co-operate, though from different motives, in a plot which the blindneſs of diſappointed ambition did not allow me to conſider with the deteſtation it deſerved: I imagined, and believe Sejanus was of the ſame opinion, that Valeria would be immediately intimidated, and accept without heſitation the propoſal of Druſus. Sejanus, unprepared for the diſcoveries of your Cheruſcan, was aſtoniſhed at the generous demeanour of

Valerius,

Valerius, when he gave the narrative of his absence to the senate; and the emperor was so much struck with his candour and magnanimity, that he began to lose his apprehensions, and even to upbraid the favourite with having falsely accused him. This alarmed Sejanus and made him endeavour to adduce pretended proofs of the designs of your uncle. The Grecian Philocles was introduced to me as a man of genius and literature, by some persons of his nation* who had a share in my education, and to whom I continued my protection. Philocles had formed, in my society, an intimacy with Sejanus; who selected him as a man proper to invent and combine such circumstances as might appear credible to Tiberius. The Greek began by insinuations, and succeeded so far in gaining the emperor's confidence, that at length he prevailed on him to believe all that

* Tacitus, Dialog. de Orat.

his

his favourite had reported: I joined in this unworthy confederacy, till I learned from Drufus that every hope of his marriage with Valeria was at an end: I then felt all the infamy of my conduct, and the remorfe of Drufus made a deep impreffion upon me: I trembled at the reflection on my guilt, and warmly remonftrated with Sejanus and Philocles on the neceffity of undeceiving the emperor. They were infenfible to entreaties, declaring that they were too far advanced to recede; and Sejanus pretended to be almoft affured that a confpiracy did exift, and would be headed by Valerius for the deftruction of the emperor and his adherents, if not timely prevented. Philocles, when left with me alone, appeared more inclined to retract his former accufations, but I am now fatally convinced of the whole extent of his perfidy. He fupped with me laft night; and the pains which will foon put an end to my exiftence, are juftly inflicted on me by the agency of a

wretch

wretch whom I have had the meanness to employ for the most treacherous purposes; he has hoped by my death to prevent the discovery of his guilt, but I have disclosed to you the criminal secret, and shall expire with less regret—if you can succeed in undeceiving Tiberius, you may still save your uncle—all access to him from me has been tried in vain."

While Aurelia was speaking, a servant arrived from Valerius, and desired me to attend him immediately: I obeyed, leaving the miserable Aurelia with assurances of my forgiveness, and her husband petrified with astonishment and horror.

I found Valerius alone; the evening was far advanced; he had been writing and held in his hand a sealed packet.

" My son," said he, " I have received intelligence of a detestable conspiracy, which, if not instantly prevented, will involve this city in flames and carnage before the appearance

pearance of to-morrow's fun. I have fent for you to carry this letter to the emperor; it contains every neceffary information, and the proofs of my fidelity. I have no doubt either of your refolution or firmnefs, to your duty; but, in times like thefe, we muft bind ourfelves by the moft folemn ties to preferve untainted the facred fpirit which fhould animate the breaft of every Roman: fwear that no confideration fhall engage you to raife a facrilegious hand againft your prince, or to difturb the tranquillity of your country."

Valerius fpoke thefe words with a dignity that feemed more than mortal: I fwore, obedient to his dictates; and he then embraced me with inexpreffible tendernefs: I related to him as briefly as poffible the awful fcene of which I had been a witnefs, and the difcovery made by the dying Aurelia. He haftened my departure: " Go, my fon," faid that excellent man, " prefent this letter: Tiberius will have no further doubt of my truth : farewell !

well! may your virtue be your guard, and every blessing attend you!"

Again he held me to his breast, and then resumed his place with his usual composure.

I went immediately to the palace, and demanded admittance, which was at first refused me, but afterwards granted, when I insisted on the immediate delivery of the letter with which I was entrusted. I found Tiberius and Sejanus in the most remote apartment of the palace. The emperor had scarcely opened the packet, and looked over the first lines, when he turned pale and trembled; he read through the contents with every token of confusion, and, taking Sejanus by the arm, led him into the adjoining room. They soon returned: their countenances were disfigured with guilt: their looks seemed directed on each other as by stealth; but they studiously avoided meeting my eyes by fixing theirs on the ground. I heard orders given for doubling the prætorian guards on duty;

Sejanus

Sejanus left the room, and returned several times, but not a word was addressed to me. It was now the fourth hour of the night, and when the emperor heard it announced by the soldiers in the court, he started from his seat as if stung by the furies. In vain I inquired whether my assistance would avail, and offered to expose my life in his defence; I repeated to him the oath which Valerius had enjoined me to take, and assured him no power on earth could compel me to violate it. He still was silent—at length the commander of the guard appeared, and whispered a few words to Sejanus, which the latter communicated to the emperor in the same manner. Tiberius yet held in his hand the letter of my uncle: he then presented it to me with these words: " Marcus, forgive me; I have been deceived;" and, immediately retiring with the minister, he closed the door upon me.

I am to this moment surprised how I survived the perusal of the letters; the first was

written

written in a hand unknown to me, and addreſſed to Valerius; it was conceived in the following terms:

" IF you wiſh to deliver your country from oppreſſive tyranny, and to vindicate the ancient rights and liberties of Rome, the glorious occaſion is now offered. This night Tiberius and Sejanus, with all their adherents, bleed in expiation of the crimes they have committed; the plot is laid with impenetrable ſecrecy; before to-morrow's dawn the palace will be in flames, and the traces of deſpotiſm effaced. If you refuſe to join us, your death, which has been already decreed by the tyrant, is inevitable; and the writer of this is charged with the execution of his ſentence. At the fourth hour of the night he will appear, and receive your final anſwer; we doubt not that you will prefer life and liberty to death and diſhonour: your memory will be for ever blaſted if you reject

our

our proffered support, and all attempts that you may make to prove your innocence will be fruitlefs. In regard to our own fafety we muft obey the emperor, and put an end to your exiftence, if you refufe to fhake off your lethargic fubmiffion, and to revenge thofe injuries that you have already endured, as well as to prevent thofe that threaten you in future."

The letter of Valerius to the emperor was as follows:

TITUS VALERIUS POPLICOLA to TIBERIUS CLAUDIUS NERO CÆSAR.

" IF the letter which I tranfmit to you is what it appears to be, you will not be affured of my fidelity till I have fealed it by my death. The principles to which I have invariably adhered, and in which every honeft citizen of Rome muft for ever agree, enjoin me to refpect in you the guardian of our laws, and the chief of our republic. I there-

fore

fore counfel you to purfue the neceffary fteps for preventing your own deftruction, and the horrors of a civil war. If, through error, you have been induced to take my life, I forgive you, and exhort you to be henceforth more wary with refpect to the choice of thofe in whom you place your confidence. If private refentment has been your inftigator, I would have you confider, that repeated acts of injuftice will weary the fufferance of Rome, and expofe you, unarmed by confcious innocence, to the refentment of your numerous enemies.

" I fend Marcus Quintius Flaminius to deliver into your hands this laft and only proof I can give of my unwearied zeal for the welfare of my country ; he is the heir of my principles, and will unchangeably and in- trepidly defend thofe characters who are held facred in Rome: I would not put his virtue to fo fevere a trial as to make him the fpectator of his parent's death, but you may com-

penfate his lofs, if you do juftice to my memory.   Farewell!"

———

The defpair that feized me after I had
read thefe letters was greater than imagination
can conceive; I had obferved the guilty
horror with which the emperor heard announced the fourth hour of night; I had remarked the confufion into which he was
thrown by the appearance of the commander
of the guard, who, I now fuppofed, had
brought him the intelligence that his mandate
was obeyed.   I flew towards the door, and
with fury would have forced it open, if, at
that inftant, Tiberius had not entered, and
affured me that Valerius lived, and that his
intended affaffin had received the punifhment
he merited.   My fenfes were confufed; I
knew not what to believe; contending
paffions had ufurped the empire of my reafon,
and I was almoft in a ftate of frenzy, when I
perceived

perceived at the furtheſt entrance of the gallery, a perſon ſurrounded by guards, whom I immediately knew to be Sigiſmar. The emperor deſired him to advance, and relate what had paſſed: he obeyed without reluctance or heſitation.

"Cæſar!" ſaid he, " I have deſtroyed the murderer of my father: I have killed him in defence of a man to whom I owe the greateſt obligations. If I am to be puniſhed for this deed, I cannot ſuffer in a nobler cauſe, though I do not boaſt of a premeditated act of juſtice: Sejanus and others whom I obſerve in this aſſembly, were preſent this day at a ſacrifice in the temple * of Hercules at Tibur ; I was there ſeen by them, and they afterwards paſſed me as they returned late this evening to the city. I received towards ſun-ſet a letter from Arminius, brought me by a meſ-ſenger whom I had diſpatched to him for

* Some remains of it are to be ſeen at Tivoli, near that of the Sibyl.

U 2

orders

orders in what manner I was to conduct myfelf with refpect to the embaffy of Ingomar.
The contents of this letter were agreeable to
my wifhes, and, being impatient to communicate them to Marcus Flaminius, I fet out
with this intention for Rome, and arrived at
his manfion when the evening was far advanced : I believe it to have been near the
fourth hour : I was informed that perhaps he
might be at the houfe of Titus Valerius, to
which place I directed my fteps ; but on enquiring for my friend, I learned that he was
abfent, and that Valerius had given exprefs
orders none fhould be admitted, except a
perfon charged with a meffage from the
emperor.   I repeated my enquiries after
Flaminius: and, during this time, I faw the
Grecian Philocles enter the portico with a
guard of foldiers : he paffed fo near me that
I inftantly recollected his features, and felt
that indignation which every man muft
feel who beholds the affaffin of his father :

he

he left the foldiers in the veftibule, and proceeded alone towards the inner apartments guided by a fervant of Valerius. I followed him, notwithftanding the endeavours of the flaves to prevent me; and, as I knew him capable of every treachery, appearances alarmed me for the uncle of my friend. I faw him enter the room where Valerius was feated near a ftatue of Rome; his arm refted on the pedeftal: ' I am come,' faid Philocles, ' to hear your final decifion; every thing is prepared, and your prefence alone is wanting to give the fignal.' Valerius anfwered coolly: ' My decifion is, I hope, already known to the emperor; you have only to execute his commands.' Philocles ftarted; but foon recovering himfelf, prefented to the fenator a bowl, which I had not before obferved. Valerius took it, and would have raifed it to his lips, when I rufhed in with precipitation, and dafhed it to the ground: at the fame inftant Philocles drew a poignard,

U 3

and

and called aloud for the affiftance of the
guard; but I wrefted the weapon from his
hand, and plunged it into his bofom: he fell,
and I furrendered myfelf prifoner to the
foldiers. Valerius addreffed them in a few
words, bidding them follow the inftructions
they had received; he faid that the part
which I had taken was wholly without his
knowledge, and contrary to his wifh, fo far
as regarded himfelf; but that having formerly
loft a father through the treachery of Philocles, the action which I had committed
was pardonable to the fudden effect of filial
refentment.

"The centurion, who commanded the
party, was furprifed and embarraffed: he
ordered his foldiers to remove the Greek,
who fhewed ftill fome remains of life; and
then turning to Valerius, told him that his
name was Herennius, and that the orphan
children of his brother, who had been killed
in Germany, were protected and fuftained

by

by Marcus Flaminius. ' I was in some measure ignorant,' continued he, ' of the purpose on which Philocles was sent. I have to reproach myself with many faults; I have squandered in vice and dissipation the patrimony which I should have shared with my nephews, yet am now sufficiently humiliated by having been chosen for this night's enterprise: but heaven forbid that I should lift my sword against the uncle of the benefactor of my family !'

" Valerius replied with astonishing serenity: ' Young man, if you are not disposed to execute the commission with which the Greek was entrusted, return to the emperor, and assure him that I have made no resistance; and that, whenever he requires it, my life is at his disposal.'

The emperor here interrupted Sigismar, by saying that Herennius had delivered to him the message from Valerius, and that he approved the conduct of the centurion. " As

to

to you, Sigifmar," continued he, " if there has been any thing reprehenfible in your conduct, it deferves to be freely pardoned in confideration of the happy confequences which have refulted from it. Valerius would wrong me to imagine that I do not fincerely rejoice in the difcovery of his innocence. As foon as I received his letter, I fent to prevent the departure of Philocles, but the commander of my guards informed me that the orders came too late."

By this time, Septimius, I recollected myfelf, and returned thanks to heaven and to Sigifmar for the prefervation of my uncle: I anfwered Tiberius, that I hoped in future he would do juftice to the virtues of a man who was fuperior to calumny and revenge, and whofe generofity in pardoning his enemies was equal to the juftice and rectitude by which his actions were invariably regulated. I then enquired whether my affiftance might not be employed againft the

infur-

insurrection which threatened the life of the emperor: his apprehensions were great, and he had already commanded that the prætorian troops should be placed to bar every avenue to the palace. A freedman of confidence was sent to examine the dying Philocles, and at his return he reported, that the Greek confessed his treasonable correspondence with the Athenian slaves in our army; and that, by their means he had formed a connexion with the remaining partisans of Clemens, the slave who successfully personated the unfortunate Posthumus Agrippa, till he was surprised and put to death by Tiberius; that finding the party was still numerous at Rome, he renewed by letter an intimacy with many of his nation, who are well received in this city on account of their talents. He employed these in reviving the hopes of the malecontents; and joined the embassy of Maroboduus, as a plausible pretence for appearing in the capital without

raising

raifing fufpicion of his defigns ; that having introduced himfelf into the familiarity of Sejanus, and into the favour of the emperor by falfe reprefentations of Valerius, he had undertaken to put him to death, the better to conceal the confpiracy in which he was himfelf engaged. He named many of the perfons who were accomplices in this odious attempt, and particularly fome of the fenators, who had lately been expelled the houfe. He however acknowledged that they would not have joined with him, but that they were made to believe Valerius approved of their defigns. It appeared that Philocles had induftrioufly fpread thefe reports of my uncle, not only at court, but amongft the confpirators, to ftrengthen by fo refpectable a name the caufe of thefe malecontents, who confifted chiefly of men of defperate fortunes and foreigners. Their meafures however feem to have been taken with fufficient precaution : Philocles, during

the

the night, was to have opened to them a private door of the palace: several of the guards were corrupted, and the emperor, his friends, and family, would undoubtedly have been massacred. Many of the chief patricians of Rome were marked out for destruction, and their effects would have been given up to plunder and rapine.

Tiberius asked what advantage the conspirators could promise themselves from the general ruin, or what system they meant to establish on so desperate an undertaking.

"The fame," answered I, "no doubt, which all conspirators have in view; that of raising their private fortunes on the public confusion; a change is all they desire, without any regard to the evils which may result from it. The true lovers of their country have ever acted in a contrary manner: the Decemvirs were expelled; the consular government was introduced by the influence of accidental events, which awakened the indignation

dignation of a long suffering people, and warned them to break the fetters of despotism; but no plots had been previously laid, no cruelty or violence attended the vindication of their liberty."

The emperor was silent, and his freedman proceeded to inform him that Philocles acknowledged he had been unwilling to communicate the plot to my uncle, for he knew the firmness of his character and feared lest he should disclose it to the emperor; but he had constantly made use of his name, and the other conspirators insisted on being certain of his concurrence, when the time of putting their project into execution so nearly approached. He flattered himself that he had obviated all danger by not disclosing it to Valerius till he supposed there could be no time for his informing Tiberius: he had placed some of the guards, who were his confederates, to prevent any message from reaching the emperor, but did not dare to trust

them with the fecret of his fatal commiffion.
Either from the conjectures of their fellow
foldiers, who were fent with Herennius, or
by fome other means, they fufpected the
intended affaffination of Valerius; and not
knowing that Philocles was the perfon employed, they imagined the confpiracy was
difcovered and confulted their own fafety by
flight. In his letter to my uncle, Philocles
had varied from his ufual hand-writing, and
at all events he imagined that by deftroying
him he fhould enfure the fecret till concealment was no longer neceffary. The unexpected death of Philocles, for he expired foon after he had avowed his crimes,
fpread a general confternation over all his
adherents: thofe who received timely intelligence of this event and of the innocence of
Valerius, fled with precipitation: amongft
thefe are the degraded fenators; the reft have
been apprehended, and will be either executed or exiled, as they appear to be more

or

or lefs guilty. The Grecian profeffors of fcience are commanded to leave the city, and many good and refpectable men, who are an honour to learning, have been confounded in this general profcription.

It is impoffible to give you an adequate idea of the humiliation apparent in the countenances of the emperor and Sejanus. The minifter endeavoured to form fome apology for himfelf, and it is evident that he was latterly deceived by Philocles, who artfully lulled his fears, after he perceived that he had fome knowledge of the confpiracy, and who perfuaded him that all would be quieted by the death of the powerful Valerius. This is but a poor extenuation of his bafenefs ; and the protection which the emperor continues to grant him is a melancholy proof that he has intrufted him with fecrets, the difclofure of which might be attended with reproach or danger to himfelf.

As foon as all in the palace was reftored

to

to peace and tranquillity, I returned with Sigifmar to the houfe of Valerius.   Our meeting was beyond meafure affecting; it feemed to be the firft time, fince my abfence in Germany, that I could feel without alloy, the fatisfaction of being reftored to him. The conftant agitation in which I had been on his account, gave place to the moft pleafing emotions, and I had the inexpreffible gratification of perceiving that he was fenfible of the happinefs of being preferved to his family.   I impatiently enquired for my Valeria, and eagerly longed to exchange our former complaints for mutual congra-.tulations.   My difquietude for her, while her father was expofed to fuch imminent danger, unfpeakably increafed my anxieties. Valerius informed me that,. when he received the letter, he was neither furprifed at the confpiracy, nor at the order for his death; and as he long expected the latter, he had fpent the greateft part of his time in

arranging

arranging every thing that might contribute to the future good of his family and friends.

" I was of opinion," said he, " from the first moment in which I had the confolation of seeing you in Ericufa, that my exiftence would be precarious, as foon as the court was apprifed of the difcovery you had made. However you confulted your duty and your affection in the fearch, and I would gladly have paid, with my life, the fatisfaction of feeing you reftored to me ; and the only chance that was left for your faving me with honour, was the determined manner in which you addreffed Tiberius, at your return from the ifland. Had not the plot been laid, of which Drufus was in great meafure the innocent caufe, it is probable either that fhame, and the fear of detection, would have induced the emperor to confent, unconditionally to your demands ; or, what I fhudder to think, that you, my dear Marcus,

would

would have been the victim of your noble sincerity and generous resentment. I should then have lost the consolation which made me look on death with indifference; Valeria would have wanted the friend and protector, whose restoration had calmed every uneasiness that I once felt for her future situation. I returned thanks to Providence for having preserved me from this misfortune, by a combination of circumstances: your reciprocal affection, and your late contract, freed my mind from disquiet, and I would not wait for my last moments to communicate to you both the advice and instructions which I thought conducive to your future honour and prosperity. The traiterous confederacy, which I learned from the letter of Philocles, delivered while you were at the house of Dolabella, convinced me that I had not been deceived in my conjectures relative to the sentiments of Tiberius and his minister. I have always believed that men are not gra-

tuitoufly wicked, however unjuft they may
be in their fufpicions. The phantoms of
the imagination are often worked up into
apparent certainties, by the infinuations of
thofe whofe intereft it is to cherifh them:
fuch has been the ftate of Tiberius, and fuch
is the perpetual delufion to which princes are
expofed. I was affured that he would repent
of my affaffination, when he received, through
my means, the information that faved his
life: I was even perfuaded that he would
prevent the blow, if I had fought my fafety
by an earlier vindication of my innocence ;
but this would have been unworthy of me,
and I did not fend for you till the time approached, in which I expected to feal, by
my death, the fidelity and candour of my
principles. You never could have wifhed
me to barter for my life, by the difcovery of
a confpiracy, which it was my duty to re-
veal ; I felt fome pain in refufing myfelf
the fatisfaction of a laft farewell to you and

to

to Valeria. Before I configned to you the packet, I had led my daughter to her apartment, and directed her to remain there, as I had bufinefs of importance to tranfact. Syrius, on whom I had conferred the gift of liberty in my laft will, was the only perfon intrufted with a knowledge of the event I expected. My commands enjoined this faithful and afflicted fervant to filence; and I gave him every neceffary direction relative to myfelf, and the laft affurances of my affection for you and Valeria. The unexpected tumult, occafioned by the fudden appearance of Sigifmar, and the fate of Philocles, alarmed Valeria, who was with difficulty reftrained, by her women, from being witnefs of a fcene ill fuited to her fenfibility. With fome difficulty I afterwards calmed the agitation into which fhe was thrown, by a relation of what had paffed; but her fears were not wholly diffipated, till a meffage from the emperor affured her of

X 2

my

my fafety, and of yours. I then obliged her to retire to reft, and wifhed to defer your meeting till her fpirits fhould be more compofed."

It was now morning, and our converfation was interrupted by the appearance of Sejanus; the natural infolence of his looks was changed into contrition and fervility; he thanked Valerius, in the moft abject manner, for the prefervation of his life, and folicited forgivenefs for a conduct, which he fought to juftify, by pretending a miftaken zeal for the fafety of the emperor.

" Sejanus," anfwered my uncle, " the prefervation of your life is a very inconfi-derable obligation; but I fhall have done you an important fervice, if the late event has engraved on your memory, that the honour and intereft of every individual are connected with the general good of the re-public. As a citizen of Rome, your ex-emption from danger affords me unfeigned
fatisfaction,

fatisfaction, and I fincerely wifh that your life may be hereafter ufeful to your country, and grateful to your prince."

You will readily imagine, Septimius, that the vifit of Sejanus was not of long duration; when he departed, I could not forbear expreffing to Valerius my indignation, that fo bafe a wretch fhould continue in the favour of Tiberius, and my apprehenfions of his future malice and indignation towards his preferver.

"You have no caufe," replied Valerius, "to apprehend any further danger for me from the malignity of Sejanus: would I were equally fure that Germanicus, and even Drufus, could be fheltered from his perfidy! It was cowardice, and not refentment, that armed him againft me. He has not fufficient delicacy to be offended by my contempt; but he feared and fought to obviate my refentment: he is at length convinced that I bear him no perfonal ani-

X 3

mofity,

mofity, and it is poffible that this may be a leffon to him, for the future, in regard to others."

Sigifmar now communicated to us the letter of Arminius. This chief not only permits, but exhorts him to remain in Italy; inveighs againft the defection of Ingomar, and the enmity of Maroboduus, and utterly difclaims any further defigns of committing hoftilities on the territories of our allies, or fuccouring the nations who may rebel againft us. He defires that Sigifmar will make known his intentions, and endeavour to prevent the fuccefs of the embaffy of Maroboduus.

My friend, whofe candour and attachment to his duty render him more capable of affifting his leader in the field, than of fupporting his intereft in political negotiations, was infinitely pleafed that an anfwer, favourable to the defires of Arminius, had been already given, and was not lefs gratified

at

at the removal of every obstacle to his settle-
ment in this country. The internal dissen-
tions of Germany are foreign to his character,
and he would neither second the designs of
his general, if aimed at absolute sovereignty,
nor draw his sword against the man whom
he has ever loved and respected.

Thus far, my dear Septimius, I have informed you of the changes that have occured.
The importance of the events, the danger
to which Valerius has been exposed, various circumstances have kept my mind,
during many hours, in a state of constant
perturbation; and I must be more composed
before I can feel the full extent of my present happiness, and my future hopes. I will
not any longer delay the sympathetic joy
you will experience. Farewell, my excellent
friend !

THE wretch who has been caft on a defert ifland, and fees no appearance of fuftenance nor means of departure, feels not fuch ecftacy at the arrival of a veffel from his native fhores, as I experience, my dear Septimius, in lofing every further apprehenfion for the fafety of Valerius, while I can yield to the tranfporting thought of being foon united to the beloved object whofe virtues make every day a deeper impreffion on my heart : the time, indeed, approaches flowly ; but no melancholy reflections now difturb the anticipation of my happinefs.

After I had finifhed my laft letter to you, I returned to Valerius, and obtained permiffion to fee his daughter ; but what words

can

can suffice to give you an idea of our meeting?

"My children," said our beloved protector, "you cannot feel more sincerely than
myself the satisfaction of my being preserved
for you.   I am fully sensible of the blessings
I enjoy, and though life has been ever considered by me as a trifle not worth our care
when compared with honour, I yet despise
the man who is indifferent to the many enjoyments and advantages of which every
thinking being is capable, or who is meanly
depressed by the difficulties and misfortunes
incident to our existence.   Neither the Stoic
nor the Epicurean seems to have discovered
the true path to happiness; it is not an
imaginary road; it is plain and simple; and
to follow it requires no other exertion than
to adhere firmly to our duty.   The man
who denies himself every innocent gratification, wants that just confidence in his own
virtue, and distrusts in himself that power
which

which should render him incapable of tref-
paffing on the limits of good and evil. He
who confiders even the moft innocent pleafures as the only objects worthy of purfuit;
who efteems it of no avail to difturb his
mind with ferious reflection, or his heart with
the diftreffes of others, expofes himfelf to a
thoufand paffions, more deftructive of tranquillity than thofe which he is fo careful to
exclude. The flighteft circumftance that
interrupts his repofe becomes to him a real
evil, and his leaft miferable moments are
thofe of uninterefting apathy.

As we attentively liftened to Valerius,
intelligence was brought us of the death of
Aurelia: fhe had languifhed out the night
with incredible torture, and expired a few
hours after the death of Philocles. It has
been difcovered that he mixed poifon in the
difhes, which he prefented to her at the fatal
fupper preceding the day allotted for the
execution of his plot: he feared detection
from

from her knowledge of his connexion with Sejanus, and wished to impose eternal silence on a transaction, which must have rendered him odious to the other conspirators.

This information renewed the horror I had felt at the sight of her sufferings. May her errors be for ever buried in oblivion! Unhappy Aurelia!

The amiable Valeria was sensibly affected with her history, and with the fatal catastrophe by which it was terminated. " I fear," said she, " that the unfortunate Aurelia has been all her life unconscious of true happiness: is it possible she never loved ?"

Need I say, my friend, with what transport I heard this remark ?

" I pity her sincerely," continued my Valeria, " she possessed exalted talents, and the power of pleasing to an eminent degree. I did not imagine that ambition had such baneful influence on our sex, who are, happily, by their education, and by the

custom

cuftom of the world, excluded from the dangerous pre-eminence that excites the emulation of men, and often impels them to actions unworthy their principles. Born to move in an humbler fphere, every diftinction is to us a danger, and celebrity the greateft of misfortunes."

Valeria expreffed the fentiments of her heart: the modefty, fimplicity, and referve of her character, drew a veil over her perfections, and render them ftill more interefting; her reading is extenfive, and her judgment far fuperior to what could be expected at her years; fhe is acquainted with the beft authors of our country, and of Greece; her exquifite fenfibility, and the livelinefs of her imagination, give her the moft correct and the moft elegant tafte for poetry. She has a general acquaintance with the fciences and liberal arts; her father having enriched her mind with a variety of inftruction which fhe ufes for the government of her life, more than for the ornament of her converfation. Her manner of fpeaking affords a ftriking example of the purity of language, which Cicero * remarked in the Roman ladies of his time, uncorrupted by the affectation, or barbarifm of foreign idioms ; all that fhe fays is dictated by truth and candor, but fhe avoids giving her opinion except fhe is earneftly requefted ; and it is eafier to fee that fhe is not ignorant of the fubject, from her attention to what is faid by others, than from any attempt to difplay her own knowledge.

Valeria is equally clear from the flighteft tincture of vanity in refpect to her perfonal attractions ; every motion is graceful, and every look engaging, but fhe appears to have been thus formed by the partial hand of nature ; and the fame exalted virtue, the fame delicacy of fentiment which regulate her conduct, illuminate her features, and animate her form with dignity and elegance.

* De Oratore.

Her

Her time is continually employed : and she never voluntarily remits her application for a moment's leifure but for the duties of affection or of urbanity.   Even when she is interrupted by the importunate vifits of the idle, she leaves them without apparent difpleafure, and always feems contented with that fociety in which she is placed.   Valeria has a general benevolence for the good, and does not confine her efteem to diftinguished talents; she never remarks a want of underftanding in innocent characters, nor fatirizes the errors of wayward imagination :   she receives the praifes of her friends not as a tribute but as a favour,. and prefers the demonftrations of regard to thofe of admiration.

After what I have faid, which is a faint picture of the virtues and graces of my Valeria, and at the fame time an unneceffary attempt to defcribe thofe perfections, which you and all who have feen her muft have obferved, will you not accufe me, Septi-

mius,

mius, of immoderate self-love, when I add, that her heart is in unison with mine, and that she has too much unaffected goodness to leave me a doubt of the sincerity of her sentiments for Marcus?

Secure of my own happiness, is it not time that I should be solicitous for yours? Why did you not sooner mention a circumstance so interesting to your friend? When I was overwhelmed with miseries and disquietude, the future prospect of your felicity would have been an alleviation to my sorrows. I have seen Atilia, who seems highly to approve your choice, and you could not form an alliance more agreeable to my wishes. The daughter of Cæcina deserves your attachment, and you are not unacquainted with my sincere esteem and veneration for her father. This brave and excellent friend of Valerius has been in Etruria since our return from Germany, but he is daily expected at Rome.

The

The reasons which still detain you in Illyria are too just for me to combat, yet how ardently do I wish for the season which may restore you to your ever grateful, and no longer unhappy friend !

LETTER

MY patience is wearied by the pompous preparations and ceremonious rites that muſt précede our marriage; and I daily complain to Valerius of the unneceſſary delay which keeps me ſtill from the promiſed happineſs. Though ſuperior to every prejudice, yet he will not depart from cuſtoms authorized by the inſtitutions of antiquity. He is of opinion that innovations are productive of worſe conſequences than may at firſt be apprehended, and in the ancient ſtructure of our laws and eſtabliſhed manners, he would preſerve the ornaments, leſt the columns ſhould fall and endanger the whole building. I often acquieſce in the propriety of theſe rules, but on this particular occaſion I could wiſh that

he were lefs fcrupuloufly attached to their obfervance.

In the mean time I have attended him to inform Tiberius of our approaching nuptials. The emperor held a long converfation with Valerius on the late events, and made num- berlefs reflections on the perils and anxieties to which the government of the republic perpetually expofed him. He declared him- felf to be, what I have ever believed him, the moft unhappy man in his dominions; but for this he affigned reafons very different from the truth. He lamented the fpirit of oppofition that pervaded the fenate, and the feditious murmurs that circulated among the people.

Valerius took this opportunity of affuring him that his difquietudes were ill-founded, and his apprehenfions ill directed. " Let us," faid he, " except a few malcontents, who have neither power nor influence as long as they are left to the neglect they deferve, and

be

be affured that the fenate and people of Rome will ever fupport the government, by which their property, their lives, and their honour are fecured. A prince has certainly greater cares, but he has alfo greater enjoyments than any other individual; his faculty of doing good is more extenfive; and when he is fully perfuaded that his own intereft and that of his country are one; that by far the majority of the people will defire his welfare and defend his perfon, while they are con-fcious that he is folicitous for their happinefs; and that the men who would excite his fuf-picions againft others are ufually themfelves the greateft traitors; fuch a prince may repofe in peace and fecurity, furrounded by a brave and generous nation, who would fuf-fer the laft extremity fooner than difturb the quiet of the ftate, or imbrue their hands in the blood of their fellow citizens. If the Roman people were diffatisfied with the prefent form of government, they would not

Y 2

fecretly

fecretly murmur, but openly throw off the yoke. If the patricians and men of fenatorial rank did not imagine that a fupreme head was neceffary for the adminiftration of affairs in our extenfive empire, they would not, from confiderations merely perfonal, content themfelves with oppofing a few decrees, but would nobly affert their original independence. Their oppofition, O Cæfar! is the fafeguard of your empire: while they attempt to ftop partial abufes, they manifeftly prove that they do not look on the general ftate of the commonwealth to be wholly defperate, and, by fupporting the ancient majefty of Rome, they add to the luftre of your imperial dignity. The beloved ruler of a free and manly people is the moft illuftrious title which a mortal can enjoy: a nation that knows by experience the united advantages of facred liberty and juft fubordination, fports, like the generous courfer, around his repofing mafter, and is ready to obey his orders when

the

the voice of glory calls him to the battle. Not so the humiliated and oppressed subjects of despotism; they drag their chains with apparent submission, but when these are once broken by chance or opposition, their long dissembled resentment bursts out with accumulated fury, resembling a beast of prey, who in the wildness of recovered liberty makes no distinction between the innocent flocks that strayed around him, or the slaves who sported with his misery. Base in his subjection, insolent and cruel in his revenge, he becomes at once a dread example to the demagogue and to the tyrant."

The emperor, though his practice had been very different, concurred in his reply with the opinion of Valerius. I foresee that they, whose duty calls them to the internal government of the republic, must live in continual warfare against the encroachments of Tiberius, and of his servile and rapacious adherents. My uncle, ever

Y 3

faithful

faithful to the conftant principles of the Valerian family, which have tranfmitted, from father to fon, the facred care of the laws promulgated by their firft conful for the fafety of the Roman people, continues unfhaken in his refolutions; happy in that firm coolnefs, and equal ferenity of temper, that fo eminently qualify him for the arduous tafk of defending the remaining bulwark of our liberties. Inferior to him in every refpect, my ardent imagination, and the impetuofity of my paffions, render me incapable of weighing, with prudence and moderation, the means of effecting what I earneftly defire. My indifcreet zeal would, I fear, be prejudicial to the caufe I endeavoured to fupport; I can neither behold with patience the man I defpife, nor liften without indignation to thofe infidious propofals which might, perhaps, be more fuccefsfully evaded by art, than rejected abruptly. A military life is the only one in which I

can

can yield to the natural impulse of my difpofition, I can there enjoy the pleafures of
fociety without a fufpicion of treachery; I
can oppofe the enemies of my country while
I efteem their courage, and when they lay
down their arms, I can become their friend
or protector. If victory and fame fhould
crown my labours, I can feel the innate
fatisfaction of having contributed to the
general good of Rome, without exciting the
hatred of any party; and whenever an inter-
miffion of martial duties reftores me to my
Valeria, not unworthy of her affection, domeftic bleffings will ftrew my path with
flowers. The friendfhips of Septimius, Sigifmar, and a few others, whofe hearts can
fympathize with us, will fhew me the
world in its faireft light. Arts, literature,
and fcience may contribute to adorn the
fortunate hours of life, and nature, in her
pureft garb, fhall prefent to us the cup of
inexhauftible happinefs.

Y 4

The

The British princes are to be prefent at the celebration of our marriage. Atilia, Cæcina, Sigifmar, now Titus, and his family, with many others of our friends, will be affembled on this occafion, and foon after we fhall fpend a few days at my villa near Tufculum.*

The Britons are infinitely pleafed with the paintings which I have defigned for their grandfather, and with fome other prefents I have been preparing for them. Mandubratius has directed them to fend him from Rome a ftatue of Germanicus. When I conducted them to the fculptor Polidore for this purpofe, I found him employed about a figure which the princes declared refembled me; and, on enquiry, I found that Valerius had, without my knowledge, ordered a ftatue of me in the attitude of a repofing warrior, with a Cupid at my feet. The artift has

* Grotta Ferrata and Frafcati.

complied with his idea, and fays the refemblance is generally thought to be exact.
When I rejoined Valerius, I could not help
expreffing my fenfe of this frefh proof of
his kindnefs: he fportively replied, that as
my unexpected return muft rob his gardens
at Baïæ of the urn, which had long been
the object of his affection, it was neceffary
that I fhould make him amends by decorat-
ing, with my image, fome part of his poffeffions.

Farewell, my dear Septimius; I am furprifed that I have not received the letter
which you promifed in your laft. What can
be the occafion of this filence?

AT length, my friend, you may congratulate the happy Marcus—Valeria is mine! No language can exprefs my ecftacy! You will not expect from me a defcription of the ceremony to which I am now reconciled, fince to that I owe the indiffoluble bond* that for ever unites me to my Valeria. Yet I muft not omit to inform you of a circumftance that will intereft you: the children of Flavius Herennius, who are educated by my directions, entreated to be two of the torch-bearers who accompany the bride to the manfion of her hufband. I willingly

* The marriages, performed with all the ceremonies, were confidered as indiffoluble.

confented,

confented, but a Flamen, who was prefent, remarked, that this office could only be performed by youths whofe father and mother were both living. The children burft into tears, and each of them running up to me, and catching faft hold of my hands, exclaimed, as with one voice, " Alas! you have made us forget that we are orphans!" I comforted them to the beft of my power, with affurance, that no Flamen could prevent them from accompanying me hereafter to the field, in the fervice of their country. I related the ftory to Valeria; fhe called them to her the next day, and prefented each of them with a jewel, in acknowledgment of their intended miniftry, and has permitted me to grant them, in her name, the fmall eftate on Mount Tufculum*, with the group of pines, cypreffes, and larch trees, adjoining to my villa.

* Still called Monte Tufculo.

We

We have already paffed three days in thefe delightful environs: they feem to have acquired innumerable beauties, which I had not before obferved; the long walks of elms and plane trees, the gentle rivulet * that murmurs through the enchanting valley, fhaded by the auguft Alban mountain, the wide extended view of Rome, the diftant fea, and the horizon adorned every evening with gold and purple by the fetting fun.— All, all, my friend, is peace, tranquillity, and delight.

A numerous and happy fociety are here affembled. Titus † is the image of cheer-fulnefs and content, and his Bertha has in fome meafure conquered the exceffive timidity, which at firft gave her an appearance of reftraint, in the midft of fo many perfons, with whofe manners and cuftoms fhe was unacquainted. Valeria, with an affability

---

* Anciently called Aqua Crabra, now La Marrana.
† Sigifmar.

peculiar

peculiar to herfelf, while fhe applauds the
artlefs behaviour of Bertha, inftructs her
imperceptibly in the modes of life unknown
to the Cherufcans.   Cæcina affures me,
that thefe are the firft days he has fpent with
pleafure fince we left the camp of Germanicus, and the happinefs of your mother
would be perfect if Septimius were added
to the company.

Lepides continues to refide at his Alban
villa, but he fees us every day, and this
morning we were furprifed, in the moft
pleafing manner, by the arrival of Manlius
Torquatus.   His friendfhip for Valerius was
the motive of his journey, and I cannot exprefs my fatisfaction in having fo favourable
an opportunity of acknowledging my obligations to him.

Nothing can equal the hilarity and eafe
with which Valerius appears in fociety: the
unremitted cares and fincere attention that
engrofs his mind, when engaged in public
busfinefs,

bufinefs, or in the ſtudies of his clofet, are
totally fufpended. now he is furrounded by
his friends. He feems to have no other
defire than to pleafe and be pleafed ; yet, in
the midſt of the gayeſt converfation, he never
fails to introduce ſome remark, or ſome example, that may form the heart, or improve
the underſtanding of his hearers. The de-
monſtrations of his affećtions to Valeria,
and myfelf, are beyond all power of expreffion.

· We have condućted the Britiſh princes to
the neighbouring villas. They have been
led through the ſtately galleries and magnificent apartments which remain a monument
of the magnificence of Lucullus*. We have
ſhewn them the ſpreading branches of the
plane tree†, under which Cicero reprefents
the eloquent Craffus giving leſſons to form

* Life ·of Lucullus, in Plutarch.
†Cicero de Oratore.

an orator, and they have feen the elegant groves * where he himfelf compofed one of the moft beautiful of his philofophical works, the favourite treatife of Septimius.

They have made further excurfions with Valerius: he yefterday accompanied them to Alba † and Aricia ‡ ; they faw the temple § of Diana, and the venerable oak ‖ : the fumptous dwelling ¶ of Pompey, and the valley ** where Ovid has fo happily given im-

* The villa of Cicero is fuppofed to have been fituated where is now the abbey of Greek monks at Grotto Ferrata.

† Palazzuolo near Albano.

‡ Laricia, fief of Prince Chigi.

§ Near the lake of Nemi, Ovid, &c.

‖ An oak is ftill fhewn, which the people of the country traditionally report to be 2000 years of age.

¶ Magnificent ruins of this ftill remain at Albano ; the convent of Maeftre Pic is built within part of the walls.

** Vallericia.

mortality to Hippolitus. On their return they vifited the hill *, which yet retains the name of Marius, and feemed peculiarly delighted with the profpect it afforded them. They talk much of the Alban lake, of the ancient ftructure † which ftill ferves for the emiffion of its fuperfluous waters, of the hiftory of Camillus, and the war of Veii, the grotto ‡ of the nymphs, and the fepulchre § of Tullia.

To-day they have been at the Portian hill ||, where dwelt the venerable cenfor: at their return they found moft of our fociety walking in the long avenue of elms, and told

* Marino fief of Prince Colonna.

† Emiffario, the emiffary of the lake of Albano, ftill in good prefervation, and built in the time of the Veian war, 397 years before the Chriftian æra.   Livy, &c.

‡ Still fhewn near the borders of the lake.

§ A tomb in the vineyard Marzelli, at Caftel Gandolpho, formerly belonging to the Jefuits, fuppofed to be that of Tullia, daughter of Cicero.

|| Still called Monte Porzio near Frafcati: belongs to Prince Borghefe.

us they had been pleafed with the fituation, but had not perceived any thing remarkable in the houfe.

"You have feen," faid Valerius, "the moft interefting fpot in this neighbourhood, the fpot which deferves to be viewed with moft exalted reverence. Art and luxury are at this time in great perfection, and even they who difapprove of their influence, yet obey the dictates of cuftom; but remember, princes, that the greatnefs of Rome does not confift in fumptuous buildings. When you firft arrived in our city you faw the Roftral column *, erected in commemoration of a glorious victory. It is fmall, and the materials of which it is compofed, are as fimple as the infcription on its pedeftal: compare it in your mind with the magnificent pyramid † of Caius Ceftius, adorned with the

* Of Duilius; at the capitol.

† Near the gate of St. Paul, at Rome.

Michael Angelo boafted that he would build in the

united excellencies of fculpture, painting, and architecture; confult the hiftory of our times, and you will fearch in vain for the actions of the man whofe afhes are there depofited. Such is the difference between the ages of virtue, and thofe of fplendor."

Torquatus here remarked that he was reconciled to the lofty monument of Ceftius, becaufe it perpetuated the remembrance of that difinterefted generofity, which induced Agrippa to reftore to the natural heirs the fortune left him by the Epulon.

"My dear Torquatus," faid Valerius, " our age can boaft of virtues not unworthy ancient Rome; and in the works of art, there are many of us who ftill prefer fimplicity and proportion to a pompous difplay of opulence; but we begin to fee coloffal figures

air an edifice equal to the Pantheon; the Cupola of St. Peters was the refult of his idea. The Vatican palace, with the gardens, &c. is faid to enclofe as much ground as the city of Turin. I am told that Mr. Byres has accurately meafured them, and found it to be true.

in

in our capital, and porticos of immeafurable length in our villas. If we fuppofe that nothing is fublime but what is immenfe, a time may come in which the Pantheon may be thought only worthy to ferve as a dome for fome gigantic edifice, and the palace of a prince may enclofe more ground than a populous city. We feem to be making fpeedy advances towards this extravagant tafle, and I leave you to judge how far it will contribute to the felicity, or real greatnefs of the people. Many works for public ufe muft neceffarily be fpacious; but it does not require any fingular genius to fubftitute magnitude for elegance and ftrength. Some voluminous hiftorians have confumed their time, and our patience, in the relation of trifling occurrences, while Cæfar alone has given the true idea of a ftile worthy the actions of a hero. In how fmall a fpace has he comprifed the moft important feries of events that ever happened on the face of the globe!

How

How clear and how diftinct is the narration ! ,

" Princes," continued he, addreffing himfelf to the Britons, " you have much to obferve and much to learn : you behold a people on whom Providence has beftowed diftinguifhed talents, and unparalleled fuccefs.   You have feen our victorious legions, and you are witneffes of our domeftic felicity.   Temperance, integrity, and courage, have been the fources of our happinefs : to thefe virtues we have owed the protection of Heaven and the empire of the world: tell me whether fuch advantages do not merit the facrifice of lawlefs pleafures, inglorious indolence, and interefted views."

At this inftant I received letters from Drufus and Germanicus : the former, who was deeply affected by the fhare he had innocently taken in the perfecution of Valerius, rejoices with me on an event which enfures the happinefs

pinefs of our family. His contrition' is undoubtedly fincere, for what other confideration could recon'cile him to the lofs of Valeria? Germanicus, with his ufual fenfibility and invariable kindnefs, congratulates me in the warmeft terms, and, O welcome, welcome tidings! informs me that you are on the road to join me. The letter that painted to you my defpair, previous to the departure of Drufus, has certainly been the motive of your benevolent vifit; you have neglected every other concern to fly to the affiftance of your friend, and you will come to enjoy his felicity.

But my Valeria approaches, the harbinger of every joy! She has feen you alight at the entrance—we hafte to meet Septimius.

F I N I S.

www.ingramcontent.com/pod-product-compliance
Lightning Source LLC
Chambersburg PA
CBHW031138120726
47905CB00006B/1736